Kick the Can

A novel
by
ANNE
CAMERON

HARBOUR PUBLISHING

HARBOUR PUBLISHING
Box 219
Madeira Park, BC V0N 2H0

Published with the assistance of the Canada Council
Cover illustration and design by Kelly Brooks
Typeset in Goudy Oldstyle
Printed and bound in Canada by Friesen Printers

Second printing December 1992

Canadian Cataloguing in Publication Data

Cameron, Anne, 1938–
 Kick the can

 Includes index.
 ISBN 1-55017-039-2

 I. Title.
PS8555.A44K5 1991   C813'.54   C91-091307-2
PR9199.3.C34K5 1991

this story is for my kids
for my grandchildren
for June Huber
and especially
for Eleanor
who has always known
Maklamaklata exists and is possible

S tories give birth to themselves, they choose their own length, their own style, and sometimes it feels as if they write themselves.

My friend June Huber, who paints haunting pictures of this coast and its soul, gave me a birthday present: six sand-scoured sea-tossed blue trading beads. I wear them with the crystal my sweetie gave me.

A month or so after I started wearing the beads, bits and pieces of this story started telling themselves to me. Rowan Hanson began talking to me, until she became more real than the 'real' people who live in this town with me.

I do not know if there was ever a village called Maklamaklata, I do not know if the people who came to introduce themselves ever lived there, I have no idea if any of the events in this story ever "really" happened

but I do believe Maklamaklata exists. In all of us; and I can only pray we all find that place and take our own kick at the can.

I

The tough-looking pregnant teen-ager in black cotton drape-shape zoot suit, pegged pants and leather motorcycle jacket, rode the bus as far as it went, then took the *Uchuk* up-coast to Zeballos. Nobody had any idea why she got off at Zeballos, but she got off and made her way up the hill from the dock, to the bar. She wasn't in the bar half an hour before she had a place lined up for a night or two. She went home with Crazy Frank and spread her sleeping bag on the floor of his stinking little shanty. Frank was so crazy everyone figured he just left the young woman alone, what with her being up the stump and all.

Next move she made was to pay for passage on a fishboat. Einarr—owner, skipper, deckhand and crew of his little putter—said he let her off at the village. Said she told him she had the name of a family she could stay with for a while, but Einarr, he couldn't remember was it the Larsons or the Hansons. It would have to be one or the other, the whole damn village was either-or and everyone related to everyone else.

She didn't look like anyone who belonged in the village, so maybe they only took her in because they felt sorry for her. You never know about those people. Or maybe she'd done a good turn for one of them and been told Anytime you're up our way drop in; that was a real possibility, and made sense to most people. There's always a dozen or so of the young ones leaving to try their hand at urban living, but most come back before very much time has passed. The few who don't should have, but there's not much use telling them that. But she moved in with some of them, and seemed to get along okay. She wasn't afraid of an outboard, she wasn't afraid to get up to her elbows in fish guts, she paid her room and board with good money and they'd have let her stay even if she'd been broke because she pulled her weight and then some when it came to work.

Tough as she was, hard-working as she was, she didn't make it through the birth of her daughter. Nobody could get her to the hospital in Tahsis because the wind was blowing ninety miles an hour, the waves were about as tall as any building anyone had ever seen, and the rain was coming down in a solid sheet. You probably couldn't have seen your hand in front of your face.

The babycatcher did what she could and she must have been damn good because the baby was fine. But the bleeding didn't stop, the afterbirth would not come out, and no matter what anybody tried, the young woman just got paler and weaker until the big Live To Ride, Ride To Live tattoo on her left arm and the Fuck 'Em If They Can't Take A Joke tattoo on her right arm stood out like beacons, looking black instead of blue against the cottage cheese of her skin.

"Is somebody singing?" she asked.

"Yes," the baby catcher assured her. "My mother and my grandmother are singing."

"Ah," she said. And later, "Who's the kid with the guitar?"

"My son," Alice smiled, her eyes bright with silver tears. "His name is Charlie." She didn't tell the young woman with the tattooed arms that Charlie had been dead for three years, crushed in a logging accident before he was seventeen years old.

"He's a nice lookin' guy," the girl whispered hoarsely. "Reminds me of a . . . a friend of mine."

"You must name your daughter," Alice urged, but the young woman seemed not to hear. She was staring out the window at the mountain ash and elderberry slapping against the glass, hammered by the force of the gale. The bright red berries reflected the light from the kerosene lamps, glistened wet with rain and looked as if they were inside the house, just a fraction out of reach.

"Oh," the young woman's eyes were glazing, "oh look, rowan berries."

"No," Alice said softly. But the tattooed child-woman sighed peacefully.

"Looks like rowan to me," she whispered, and since she didn't say another thing after that, they decided to call her daughter Rowan. It sounded close to a traditional name the babycatcher's family owned, and what with the painted woman having heard the singing and actually seeing Charlie, and he'd been playing music to help her on her way over, they all decided that even if she didn't look the least bit like any of them, she must be related somewhere. They talked it over and decided she was probably a Hanson, but they weren't exactly sure of that. If she was a Hanson, it was up to the Larsons to bury her; if she'd been a Larson, the Hansons would have had the honour. Not knowing for sure, they both did what needed to be done, and if it wasn't exactly how it had been done since Forever, what the hell, everything was changing and if you can't adapt you disappear.

The afterbirth slid out after the young woman was dead. That was strange. They talked about it over pots of tea. Afterbirth is very important. It's not something you just toss to the dogs, or burn in the fire, or throw away in the garbage. Without afterbirth there is no connection between male and female, no child happens, no soul is invited from the Otherworld, no miracle occurs. Afterbirth is like the bridge between real and magic, between this life and the other, between here and wherever the young woman had gone to be with Charlie and the others. Just as a rainbow is the bridge between earth and sky, and to prove it, all you have to do is believe the evidence of your own eyes, look at the afterbirth, see the rainbow sheen to the skin covering of it, and let faith grow.

It was a good thing, though, when you thought about it. Maybe if she'd been buried with the afterbirth still inside her the child would have left, too. That had happened more than once. The soul is connected, after all, to the afterbirth and if it doesn't stay here how can the soul stay here?

They talked until dawn, and then, when the sky began to go from black to pearly grey, they took the afterbirth and went out into the rain with it. The men had dug where they had been told to dig and the hole was ready, lined with cedar and sage. They put the glistening sack carefully in its place, then covered it with more cedar, both red and yellow, and with arbutus leaves and some arbutus bark, as was proper and fitting.

Since she was to be a Hanson, it was they who started the ceremony, but because she was obviously related to the Larsons, and who wasn't in that village, it was the babycatcher who recited the identification prayer and sprinkled salt water, to tie the child to the sea. The old man brought out his eagle feather and dipped it in fresh water, then sprinkled that on the afterbirth, too, so the child would cherish clean water. They smudged with Old Grandmother, and then, before they filled in the hole, they went back to the house and got the baby, and brought her, naked, with the rain washing her body and the first light of full day shining on her. They cut a bit of her hair and put it in with the placenta, and added a lock of her mother's hair so she would know in her heart what every child needs to know about her mama. Then they filled in the hole, taking turns, each of them praying the proper prayers, binding the child forever to the coast, dedicating her to a life of propriety. The giving of the afterbirth to the earth is a giving back to the Mother of All, a promise that we will take of Her bounty that which we need to survive, but we will always give back to her and treat her with honour. When we are dead we will be given back to her, to rejoin our placentas, which we gave freely even before we had tasted of the plenitude of this earth.

They did not mark the spot. That spot is not something for us to mark and know and visit. It must be given freely, so that for the rest of our lives, wherever we go on this earth, we know the blood and fibre of our first connection has been absorbed and welcomed by the very one who will nourish us, and she is the Earth, and we are at home on her however far we are from the places we know.

"Rowan Hanson," the old blind granny said, "you are part of this place forever. You are part of us forever. We are yours and you are ours. Live with honour and die when it is time."

They took her back into the house, then, and let her see who her mother had been. Just to be sure there was no confusion, Anthony Larson got out paper and pencil and copied the tattoos. Not just the ones on the arm. He copied the unicorn on her shoulder and the rose above her breast, he even copied the Born To Boogie on her thigh and the Willingdon Women on her back.

Alice's cousin's second oldest daughter was nursing a baby and had enough milk to feed Rowan, too. Since she was feeding two, everyone took over her other chores, so all she had to do was sit and keep those two souls alive. It was funny to look at, though. Louie Larson was almost thirty pounds, with thick straight black hair and squint-shutty eyes and Rowan Hanson had dry-grass hair and eyes almost as round as a seal's eyes. And she was much smaller because she was months newer.

Nobody knew the real name of the dead mother, and Bugsie is like no name at all even if that is what she had told them to call her, but the dead don't own names any more anyway, so it didn't matter. They buried her properly and put a prayer on her belongings. Ordinarily, the belongings would have been burned, so she wouldn't stay tied to them and maybe come back and ghost people, but times change, and they all knew sooner or later the Mountie would be around to check up on things and ask questions. It was unsettling to have belongings from a deader stored in a box. Even with strong prayers you just never know, but the young dead woman with no name and so many tattoos must have been properly raised and must have died with her thoughts in order, because she stayed gone and never bothered anyone.

The Mountie came, eventually, with no questions about anything important. He asked if there were any problems, and people said no, no problems, so he stayed long enough to fill his belly with baked salmon, then went back to his launch and headed off to check on things somewhere else.

The seasons moved smoothly from warm to cold, from dry to wet, and Rowan tucked her feet under her, stood upright, and made her way out into the wider world. She laughed, she ate, she slept, she began to talk, and she usually fell asleep on Alice's lap, cuddled against the warm bulk of the woman she considered to be her mother.

Every month the government sent someone to Brighton Bay to take care of things like inoculations and to make arrangements to have people with toothache flown out to the dentist. Anyone who needed help any faster than that could always Mickey Mouse radio for help, but usually people waited until the government people were due to show up, then took a fishboat ride the ten miles or so to have their needs seen to. Once a week the steamer docked briefly to offload the mail and whatever groceries or other freight was being brought in from Outside. Things might have gone properly except the motor of the float plane taking the government man to Brighton Bay started coughing and choking and the pilot put it down in the bay, which just goes to prove anything anybody ever suspected about machinery and what a mess it can make in a person's life.

Riding in the float plane was the welfare guy. And he couldn't just sit out there bobbing in the bay for the two and a half days it took for another plane to arrive with a mechanic and spare parts and all that business. No, he had to have food and a place to sleep. He saw Rowan Hanson racing around in red gumboots and blue shorts, her straw-hair long and shaggy, her sea-changing eyes bright in her golden tan face. Those eyes weren't as round as a seal's any more, probably the milk she had slurped and guzzled had changed her a bit because her eyes tried to slant, but didn't quite make it, just turned down some at the outer corners. The welfare guy, he said that probably meant she was part Scotsman, but the Scotsman family lived up-coast three hours by fishboat and hadn't had anything to do with any of it.

"She can't stay here," he said. Even knowing the story, even knowing all about everything, he insisted she didn't belong. When he went, he took the box of belongings and he took the drawings Anthony Larson had made. Even worse, he took Rowan Hanson with him.

The whole village showed up for the hearing. They closed down the smokehouses and everything. Rode out on fishboats and turned up in their best clothes at the courthouse, and one by one they gave witness and testimony. "No," said the honourable one in the black robe, the one who sat up behind the big polished wood desk and listened with a polite attention nobody had any reason to expect from an Outsider. "No," he repeated, and he gave reasons that made no sense to anybody. He didn't even care about the milk changing the shape of her eyes or the afterbirth being buried where you could see the water heaving down at the foot of the cliff. "No."

They almost made a dreadful mistake. They almost went home and held a funeral. It would have made sense. Rowan Hanson was gone from them and none of the children who had been taken in the past had ever come back again and most of them died within months of being taken away. But Alice was a woman who hung on until long after the last dog had been hung. "No," she said stubbornly, "Rowan Hanson is alive! And I will *not* stop using her name. I will *not* stop praying for her!"

So they didn't have the funeral. And Alice made sure the stuff the welfare guy hadn't taken was put out where everyone could see it and be reminded all the time that Rowan Hanson was alive and well and doing just fine thank you. Every morning Alice said her prayers and mentioned the name of Rowan Hanson, and every night before she went to bed she made a pot of tea and drank a cup of it looking out at the place where the float plane had disappeared in the sky, and she thought hard about that child. Then she poured the rest of the tea on the ground beside her front steps so that if Rowan Hanson wanted to, she could come for her share of the tea, and then she'd be at the foot of the stairs and Alice could snatch her up and keep her where she ought to never have been taken from, except for the bad luck because of the machinery which never worked right when you wanted it to anyway.

II

Since the only name they had for the toddler was Rowan Hanson, that was the name they put on the forms, and that was the name the foster mother used when she spoke to the child. "Rowan," she would say, "Rowan, honey, come get your face washed." "Rowan, time for lunch."

The Mounties checked their files and the tattoos did it for them. Carol Milligan. Turned out the Willingdon Women tattoo was the oldest, put on when she was fourteen and incarcerated in Willingdon School for Girls. Put there because she was "incorrigible." Chronic runaway. Truant. She broke out of Willingdon when she was fifteen and collected the Born to Boogie between then and when she was arrested the next time.

"A fast, hard, short life," her mother sighed. "But she's at rest, now, I hope."

Rowan Hanson was kept in the foster home because, after all, Mary Milligan wasn't exactly the one you'd give a two-and-a-half-year-old kid to look after. Some called that kind of woman a Bunkhouse Diana, some said Bunkhouse Betty, some said Loggers' Whore and some said Floatcamp Floozie. Small wonder Carol Milligan had wound up where she had wound up as young as she'd been when she got there.

But Mary Milligan wasn't bad, or cold, or heartless, or mean. She just had a different line of work than some people found acceptable.

She took her days off according to the cycles of the moon, and every month showed up in Extension for four days, demanding to see her granddaughter. "I got my rights," she said firmly, "and you know I do."

Mary Milligan knew all about what had happened. She might not know how to behave, but she knew how to be. "Rowan Milligan my foot," she laughed, "Rowan Hanson if you don't mind!" Nobody paid any attention at the time.

The foster mother in Extension suddenly found herself pregnant. She was amazed. She was enthralled. She ran an ad in the paper thanking St. Jude the patron saint of hopeless causes.

"Oh, I've prayed for years," she wept joyously. "We tried everything and finally applied to adopt, but the waiting list is so long and it just takes forever, so that's when we started fostering." And she scooped up Rowan Hanson, cuddled her tightly, and said, "You're the one brought the good luck with you when you came. Give me a big smooch, you darling you."

Rowan was moved to a different foster home. Not so much because the fostering parents didn't want her, but because it was policy at the time not to leave a child in one place long enough for it to make strong attachments to people who were not natural or even adoptive parents. Sooner or later the kids would have to move on, so might as well move them before they'd sunk their roots in too deep. It was also policy that foster children had to be younger than natural children in the family, so as not to pre-empt anyone in the natural family pecking order.

Not one educated asshole ever bothered to think about it in terms of a lilac tree. You can't dig 'em up and move 'em every fifteen months and expect them to bloom and flourish.

By the time she was seven, Rowan had been in four foster homes and she was feeling definitely rootless and upset. "I don't like moving," she told Mary. "It's always a different class in a different school with different teachers and different streets to walk to get back to the house. And when you get there it's different people and different rules."

"What would you like?" Mary asked.

"I would like to be able to know the people who live next door and across the street," Rowan admitted shyly. "I'd like to know what dogs growl and what dogs are nice. Just . . . like that. You know."

Mary didn't talk much about what she was thinking and feeling, but she'd been doing a lot of both ever since they told her Carol had wound up dying in some frog pond of a place the name of which nobody seemed able to pronounce. She knew she hadn't done as well by the kid as she could have, and certainly not as well as she should have. But shoulds and coulds didn't count in that area any more. All she could do was look at how things had come down and try to take responsibility, and she had a lot of that to take.

Mary knew nobody was going to turn a kid over to a Floatcamp Floozie. She had a few good years left to her; she'd only been fifteen when Carol was born and hadn't had to blow out her forty candles yet, but she'd learned the hard way how many chances get taken away from you before you get around to taking advantage of them.

Mary packed her bags and moved to town. She rented the top floor of a three-storey pillar of a house halfway up the hill from Commercial Street. There was a little bit of a fire escape balcony off the kitchen and you could sit there with a cool beer on a hot day and look out over the harbour and think about all the things there were to think about in your life. Mary Milligan had a lot to think about, some of it the kind of stuff she'd been trying for years to drop to the bottom of an ocean of beer. Most of what she'd gone and chewed she could swallow, even if it did kind of stick in her throat, but there were some lumps she had never been able to get down or spit out, and she had to come to terms with them on that balcony fire escape. She'd never intended to be a mother, but she'd wound up being one and she'd blown it all to hell. She'd never intended to be a grandmother, either, but here she was, and blowing this one all to hell seemed like a fast way to wind up on the sizzling hobs herself. There's no big sin in making a mistake but only a dipper makes the same one more than two or three times.

When she was settled into that groove she got herself a job as a short-order cook. She'd cooked in enough camps of one kind or another for enough years she could short-order with one hand tied behind her back and a grin on her face. She didn't go to AA or any of that, she just did what she'd said all along she could do, quit any goddamn time she had a mind to quit. Of course it wasn't as easy as that, but Mary Milligan wasn't one to cry her sad song in anyone else's ears. She'd known enough dry alkies and heard enough of their stories to know you can't half quit the booze, you quit, and to do that you have to stay away from the places you're used to going, and stay away from the people you've been most at home with all your life. She knew before she took the deep breath prior to the plunge just how bitchin' miserable it was going to be, but she also knew she'd been telling the truth when she said she could quit any time she was of a mind to quit.

And she waited. Every weekend she saw Rowan, and then she got to where they let her have the kid with her on Saturday overnight. She took the bus to the foster home, and the kid was waiting at the bus stop, almost coming out of her skin with excitement. "C'mon," Mary called, and Rowan raced onto the bus. No hugs or kisses or smooches, just big grins, and they rode the rest of the route in to town together. There was always more to do than there was time to do it in, and when it was done, they'd go for Chinese food and a movie after, then walk up the hill to the tall skinny house.

"This is real nice," Rowan approved. "I really like this."

"Me, too, Smoocherooni."

"Yeah, Smoocherooni-you!" the kid laughed and kissed the air between them. It wasn't much, but god it went a long long way to healing all the old crap.

Not just Mary Milligan's crap, either. Rowan Hanson had need of some healing, too. Taken into care before she was three years old, taken from people who considered it a gift to scoop up a small person and blow giggles against her small neck, she was handed over to workers whose case loads were too big for them to get to know their charges, and she was put to live with people who got paid for putting up with her. Not all the foster parents were kind, not all were loving, and each had a different way of doing things. By the time she was seven, Rowan Hanson had been in more foster homes than she would ever remember and not all of her experiences were good, or even acceptable. For a long time she wasn't even sure her grandmother would remain in her life. What if the Saturday bus arrived and was empty? What if the driver looked at her with disinterested eyes, then closed the door and drove off, leaving her on the sidewalk? What if she got on the bus and it just drove away with her, up and down streets she had never seen, back and forth, back and forth forever and ever, and nobody on it but her, all alone with someone else deciding whether they'd ever stop or not, whether they'd ever go back to the street she knew?

But Mary Milligan was on the bus every Saturday. She was standing in the aisle at the top of the steps, smiling and wiggling her hand in a little wave. "C'mon," she said. Every Saturday, "C'mon," and the surge of relief was so strong Rowan felt as if she was going to cry, and then it came out of her throat as a laugh.

Sunday nights, when she was back at the foster home and lying in the bed they had given her to use, she would think back over every single thing they had done together, then store the memories away, to be brought out again and again, always when she was alone. Not once did she offer any of it to anyone else, not for Show And Tell, not for How I Spent My Vacation, not for anything or anybody. Too much of her life had been shared, too many times her precious stuff had been packed by other people, moved by other people, unpacked by other people, put in drawers or boxes by other people, then examined by other people. "Oh, let me see. Where'd you get that? Can I borrow it some time?" and you always had to say yes, because it was important you learn to share, and not nice to be selfish. But she wasn't going to share her Saturday sleep-overs with anybody else. They were just about the only things she had that were hers, and she might need them someday. The bus might stop and Gran might not be on it, and then Rowan would need every happy memory she'd saved just to keep from falling into a big black hole.

By springtime Rowan was eight, and Mary could have her from Friday night when school let out until Sunday night at bedtime.

"If I rent a house, with a yard and all," she asked, almost idly because it doesn't pay to let them know how much things mean to you, "would Rowan be able to live with me?"

"Are you sure you're ready for it?" the worker asked.

"Oh, I think so," Mary nodded. "Think she is?"

"Oh, I'm pretty sure she is." The worker had no illusions about Mary Milligan and her past life, nor about the present life, either. She knew Mary had spent more than half her lifetime being, as they say, no better than she ought to be, but she also knew Mary had quit the booze and found what the forms called steady gainful employment. She might not be the ideal parenting figure, but she was better than none, and she'd hung in longer than the fly-by-night stuck-with-temporary-guilt part-timers would have. It might not have been the kind of reformation made the Evangelicals hold their hands high and weep for joy at a soul saved from damnation, but it was better than most could have accomplished and it would do just fine by her.

They went house-hunting together, which was only fair since they both had to live in it. They settled on a place the owner called two-bedroom and they called bedroom-and-a-half. "You can have the bigger room," Mary said, "you've got toys and all that stuff and all I have is a body that has to lie down on a bed at night."

"Oh, I could have the half," Rowan suggested. "I'm smaller."

"Yeah, but you might want to have friends sleep over," Mary countered, "and I have pretty well done that as often as I need." She smiled, and rumpled Rowan's sun-streaked hair, and the wide grin on the kid's face was suddenly more than Mary could look at, because it made her eyes fill with water. She knew if the Duke of York showed up wanting to stay overnight she'd hand him a bus ticket to somewhere else. And she knew without any sense of shame, sorrow or loss that ninety-six per cent of those who had stayed overnight, or over several nights, or even over the nights of fire season or snow shutdown, had meant absolutely zip all to her, and the staying had meant about that to them, too. The knowledge didn't make Mary feel cheap, or diminished, it was just calm realization and, in its own way, healing. Like the booze, she could quit any time she was of a mind to, and she was of a mind to do just that, so she did.

They dug flowerbeds and planted flowers, the names of which Mary might once have known but had now forgotten. "I don't know," she admitted, "but they grow in all the yards where people have put down roots and decided to stay put. Primroses, maybe. Very English, anyhow."

"I like the light yellow ones best. They look like butter."

"What would you know about butter, a kid as has been raised on margarine?"

"What does that mean?" Rowan asked. Mary laughed and promised one day it wouldn't need explaining. "Why do you suppose," the child asked carefully, "my mother didn't want to live with me?"

"Whatever gave you that idea?" Mary stopped digging and gratefully eased the crick in the small of her back.

"Well, where is she, then?"

Mary gave it to her straight. "She's dead."

Rowan stared off past the yard, past the fringe of trees to where the creek burbled over the rocks. "She died when you were brand new."

"Did I kill her?" Rowan dared.

"No. Things happen. And I know that's not much of an explanation, but it's about as good as I can do because there's things I don't understand, either."

"You're sure I didn't kill her?"

"Darling, I am positive you didn't kill her. You were brand new, and your hands weren't any bigger than these flowers will be when they open, so how could you have killed her? People die. Some people don't do that until they are old, old, old, and other people do it when they're still young. One day I'll die. One day you'll die. And it doesn't really matter when you die, or even how you die, you'll die. It's what you do with the time in between the being born and the being dead that counts."

"If she hadn't died, would she have wanted me?"

Mary looked at the kid and nodded, smiling widely. And didn't feel the slightest twinge of guilt for the lie she might be telling. In all probability, Carol wouldn't have been any better at being a mother than Mary herself had been. In all probability, Carol would have made every silly damned mistake that could be made. Dragged the kid up in slum rooms in the skid end of town, fed her Krap Dinner and wieners, never had money for dentists because it had been blown on beer or on whatever it was they poked up their noses or into their veins. None of which meant she hadn't wanted the kid. All that stuff has little or nothing to do with want or love, it's just the gift that goes on giving, from generation to generation, living out the nutsiness that was lived out on us, and few of us as smart at sixteen as we will be at thirty-six, or as smart at thirty-six as we will be at fifty-six.

"Your mother was *nuts* about you even before you were born," she said, and it was probably true. Carol had been pretty nuts most of her life.

They went for a walk together, hand in hand along the little dusty road that passed in front of the rented house. Mary didn't try to pad any sharp corners or smooth any rough edges, she told Rowan what little she herself knew.

"Maklamaklata?" Rowan puzzled. "What an odd name. What does it mean?"

"I don't know. I'm not even for-sure sure that's what it's called. It's what it sounded like when they told me. We could look for it on the map."

They looked. Didn't find it. Found other places with strange names; CeePeeCee and Clo-Ose and names even stranger, but no Maklamaklata. They even checked at the post office but nobody there knew much. "Probably they hardly know where Saskabush is," Mary grumbled when they were back on the street again. Nobody had mentioned Brighton Bay, which they could have found, and nobody had bothered mentioning Scuttle Bay, which was what the village had been renamed by the first outsiders who made a map. The only reason any of them had known Maklamaklata was that the Mountie, who was originally a farm kid from Ontario, liked to drop little-known names to prove he had some kind of understanding of the coast and its people.

They dropped it for a while and then Rowan picked it up again. "Why did my little mother go off like she did? Why didn't she stay with you?"

"We had a fight," Mary admitted sadly.

"What about?"

"You know, the truth of it is, I don't even remember. Some stupid little count-for-nothing thing that got blown all out of proportion. Whatever it was, it wasn't worth everything that came down because of it."

"Don't let's us have fights, okay?"

"Fine by me, kiddo. Whatever your little heart desires."

"My little heart desires a new car and a million dollars."

"Your little heart will break, I guess," Mary shrugged. Rowan shrugged. Then they both laughed.

"How is it working out?" the welfare woman asked.

"Hunky-dory," Mary answered easily. "Wish I'd'a been this smart the first time around. Some people," it was as close to an apology or a confession as she would ever make, "learn fast and others learn the hard way. I guess I never learned fast."

Rowan turned nine in the little rented house, then turned ten and was on her way toward eleven when the landlord drove out to hand them the paper. "My kid is getting married," he apologized, "so her'n the jerk'll be moving in here. Sorry and all, but . . . blood and water, you know how it is."

"Sure," Mary Milligan agreed. "Proper thing, too."

"Wish she wouldn't marry him," the landlord mourned, "he's a right lugan, one of them walking advertisements for birth control, you know the type. Useless as tits on a panda bear. Makes it all the more important that she live here. Can't be sure the dumb shit will even be able to pay rent on a bait-box! I'd sign the place over but that'd give him half interest in it and goddamn if I'm giving *him* anything!." He sighed deeply, then his face went as red as blackberry juice. "She's up a stump," he confessed.

"Oh well," Mary shrugged, "you wait until the baby comes. You can't hold a child's father against the child. Otherwise we'd all have been writ off long ago." They both laughed. "Bein' a grandparent," Mary promised, "is one helluva lot better'n bein' a parent ever was. Take it from one who knows."

The landlord felt a lot better when he left. He wished he could have found some other way than giving them notice, but there wasn't any he could see and you had to put your own first, even the Bible said charity begins at home.

They found another place, but not at the same price. It was two full bedrooms but no real yard, just a bit of grass in the back, and no use trying for flower beds because the downstairs people had four little kids and a lot of friends who showed up on motorcycles which they parked any old where at all any hour of the day or night. There was an incredible amount of coming and going, to-ing and fro-ing, and at first Mary thought the downstairs neighbours were bootlegging. When she found out what it was they were really selling, she started looking all over again for a place to rent.

"By me," she muttered to the dishes in the sink, "any scumsucker who sells dope ought to be hung by his balls to dry to death in the summer sunshine."

The next place was on the ground floor, in back, with a strip of hard-packed earth between the steps and the rickety falling-down fence that was supposed to divide the property from the alley. The five other families in the big green house put their garbage in the dented cans along the back fence and the truck came every Tuesday just after first light, to collect trash and waken the world with clattering and banging. Any time anyone in the house flushed the john, the pipes in Mary's place rattled and gurgled. If someone else had a bath you knew about it because of the slamming and humming in the plumbing. Footsteps echoed as clearly as if the neighbours were walking in your sinus cavities, and there wasn't an aspect of marital life that was unknown to Rowan by the time she was eleven.

They went to the courthouse that year and sat on polished benches waiting for their names to be called. The magistrate or judge or stipendiary or whatever in hell he was, listened to what the welfare worker had to say, then he signed something and that was it, the welfare was out of the picture and Mary Milligan had full custody.

"Does that mean I'm yours?" Rowan asked quietly.

"All mine," Mary agreed. "I can sell you to the tinkers, now, if I want."

"Guess you'd get a good price," Rowan laughed. "They buy by the pound, don't they?"

"Sure do. Get more for you if you had some talent of some kind. Music or dance or whatever. If you'd even learn to clatter a coupla spoons together in time to the beat we'd get a better price but the only spoon clattering you do is against the side of the soup bowl and they don't pay extra for appetite." She slid her arm around Rowan's shoulders, gave her a brief, tight hug. "Come on, Smoocherooni, let's go celebrate with fish'n'chips, okay?"

"Okay, Smoocheroni-you," Rowan agreed.

Rowan headed off to school at eight-thirty every morning, an hour after Mary had headed off to work the grill at the Black Cat Cafe. School went in at nine, broke at noon for lunch, went in again at one, and was over for the day by three-thirty. Rowan was home by four and Mary arrived between four-thirty and five. The first thing she did was run a hot bath and get into it to scrub away the smell of stale grease. "Goddamn," she sighed, "after a while it gets right into your skin. No wonder the bloody dogs chase me down the street, they think I'm a hamburger patty."

"Patty or paté?" Rowan teased.

"Patty," Mary winked, "although there's some says Paddy, because of being Irish."

"What's s-l-o-u-g-h?" Rowan asked. "It means, like a swamp. How does a person say it? Slew? Sluff?"

"I've heard it said slew." Mary ducked her head under the bathwater to rinse shampoo suds from her tight-permed hair. "Mostly by back-easters. Mostly, though, what I've heard sounds like how to say bough, like the branch on a tree. Slough. Never heard sluff. You might look it up in the diction-whoozis."

"I can't understand all those wiggles and marks they use to tell you how to pronounce things. Can never remember if the hard C says kuh or see. Is a hard G the guh or juh or the gee or...and how are you supposed to use a dictionary to find out about a word if you don't know how to spell it in the first place?"

"Don't ask me. The best part of school for me was recess, lunch time, and finished. Hand me that creme rinse, will you? Thanks. What's all the puzzle about slough, anyway?"

"Despond," Rowan explained. "They talked about the slough of despond."

"Well, how did *they* say it?"

"They didn't *say* it. It was in a book. The Slough of Despond. And I wasn't sure how you'd say it out loud."

"Well, prob'ly not sluff. Despond means sad, and sluff, that's more like rotting off."

"Words are funny, eh?"

"Yeah. Lots of stuff is funny. Me sittin' here going blue with cold while you talk on about sluffs of despond, that's funny. Why don't you go push the kettle onto the heat and I'll get my old bones dry and start supper."

"Sluff," Rowan agreed. "Sluff, slough, slew, sluff slough slew," and chanting softly she went into the kitchen to do her part toward getting supper thrown together.

The coast goes boom and then it goes bust. Since the first patch-ass dispossessed arrived to claim what had never been theirs, the economy soared and dove in unpredictable swings amazingly similar to premenstrual tension. In boom time the towns fill up with outsiders who arrive in heavy-booted droves to run survey lines, hammer stakes, flatten hills, fill valleys and lay blacktop where there is no sane reason for a road, so other outsiders can come in and shave the forests, or excavate ugly open pits from which are hauled away the minerals that enrich the members of the board of directors, all of whom live as far from the scene of carnage as geographically possible. In bust times all the outsiders head back to where they came from and only the bitter-eyed locals are left to scratch and scrabble as best they can, killing time and passing their lives numbly, waiting for the next boom.

The Black Cat Cafe went from being jammed eighteen hours out of twenty-four to barely making enough to pay the electricity bill on the flashing sign over the door. The red plastic-covered stools were re-covered, the black paint touched up on the metal legs of the booths and tables, the chipped and stained arborite countertop was blowtorched off and a new one put down, but none of it improved business. Mary Milligan wasn't the least bit surprised when the owner dropped by to give her the bad news.

When he slid onto the stool without saying anything, Mary slid a cup of coffee and a slice of lemon pie in front of him. He nodded thanks, added sugar and cream, stirred, then put his spoon on his saucer and picked up the fork to take a dive at the pie. Their eyes met, and Mary nodded.

"Hell, Mary," he whispered, "I'm sorry as all get-out, but. . ."

"Hey." She untied her apron, put it on the shelf behind the counter, got herself a piece of pumpkin pie and a cup of coffee and moved to sit on the stool next to the boss. "It lasted about three months longer than made sense, Blackie."

"It's a bitch," he agreed.

"You been carrying me, and I appreciate it." She tasted the pie she had baked herself, and nodded approval. "Thank God for pogey," she grinned. "But you, you dumb bugger, you don't get it. That's because," she teased, "you're one of them capitalist pigs."

"Yeah," he agreed, "Me and Daddy Warbucks, right?"

Pogey is supposed to tide a body over between jobs. Pogey is supposed to be insurance against economic downturn. Pogey is supposed to be a safety net. It isn't supposed to be a way of life. And because it isn't supposed to be a way of life, the pogey rate is never set high enough to properly sustain life, it just keeps body and soul together until another job can be found. In downturn time there are no jobs to find. Mary checked Manpower, she checked the papers, she went once a week to every place in town, and she collected pogey. It paid the rent, it bought food, but when Rowan's sneakers wore out Mary had to dip into her pathetically small savings. She waited until Rowan was in bed and asleep, then sat at the kitchen table looking at the sneakers neatly left by the space heater. Just ordinary rubber-soled canvas-topped sneakers, hardly worth picking up and taking home, certainly not the leather high-tops the kid probably really wanted. Cheapos, guaranteed to wear out over the big toe, guaranteed to develop holes over the small toe, guaranteed to rip where the top joined the sole.

Mary went into the pantry and took a look at the food on the shelves. She went back to the kitchen table and rolled a cigarette, then glared at it as if it were to blame for not being a tailor-made. She lit up, inhaled and squinted past her own smoke. As long as she'd been working at the Black Cat she'd had her main meal of the day free gratis and had often brought home the last of the meatloaf or the leftover luncheon special. She'd had an apron pocket heavy with tips, and if her paycheque was small, it was better than pogey. Now things were starting to look mean. The kid was starting to do the kind of bullshit things Mary remembered doing when she was a kid, saying she wasn't hungry when you knew damn well she was, saying she wanted canvas cheapos when you knew she'd really rather go barefoot.

Mary finished her rollie, then went into the bathroom. Fifteen minutes later she came out with her chenille bathrobe belted around her waist. She went to her bedroom, closed the door and ten minutes later came out dressed in her best polyester slacks, with a white ruffle-front blouse and her good patent leather low-heels on her feet. She was wearing all her war paint, and the big rings she hadn't worn since she'd made her decision about Rowan only those few years ago. She checked herself in the mirror over the basin, nodded grimly, and headed out the back door.

Where she went, who she met, and what she did were nobody's business but her own, and she was back home, ungeared, war paint washed off and smiling when Rowan wakened in the morning. Mary cooked up bacon, eggs, and toast, made sure the kid was full, kissed her on both cheeks and saw her off to school with her bag lunch and homework in her pack. Then Mary took herself off to bed and slept until the alarm went off. When Rowan came home from school, she was up, face washed, dressed, and looking great. "How was your day?" Mary asked. "Learn anything at school?"

"Not much. How was your day?"

"Oh, pretty much like a coupla thousand others I remember."

And that night, when Rowan was in bed and sound asleep, Mary did 'er again, got herself dressed to the nines, tacked and spray-bombed her hair in place, put her big shiny rings on her fingers, then headed off to that place where more jobs are found than Manpower ever hears about. Mary bought her own first beer, but no sooner was it in her hand than a second-loader she'd known in a camp near Juskatla a few years back was waving her over, a broad grin on his face. "Hey, there," she smiled, "and who you don't see when you've got no gun. How'n hell ya doin'?"

"So-so, like always. Yourself?"

"Fine as silk," she lied.

Three weeks later she broke the news to Rowan. The kid sat at the supper table busy with two hamburger patties, onion gravy, mashed potatoes and mixed vegetables, listening carefully and nodding, big-eyed and serious.

"It means moving," Mary explained. "And it means you won't be going to a regular school. Some of the other mothers will supervise correspondence courses for you instead. I won't be much help there," she confessed. "You've gone further already than I ever did."

"Sounds. . . different," Rowan said carefully. "But it sounds okay."

"Every now'n again there's a boat comes by," Mary elaborated, "a kind of travelling library. You can get a whole boxa books to tide you over until next time it comes. They said they had a satellite dish, so that's something. It's a bitch, kid, I know, but. . ." She shrugged.

The kid grinned and Mary could have put her head on the oilcloth table cover and wept hot salty tears. So much for trying to make plans, so much for trying to live how you've never lived, so much for cleaning up the old act and pulling all the shit together and acting normal. No use trying to pretend to be who you aren't, no use trying to pass for someone you were never intended to be. When the best jobs of your life have been come by because you were in the pub at the right time and had sense enough to recognize opportunity by its half-drunken knock, you learn to take what you can reach out and grab ahold of and you learn not to look a gift horse in the mouth. After all, she'd put on her war paint and headed for the suds shop knowing full well what it would lead to. A fuckin' job, is what! And if it wasn't glamorous, if it wasn't even exactly enviable or even respectable, what did that matter? Why do you suppose they call it work? It's not supposed to be fun. Play is fun. Work is just work and most of the time it's rotten, lousy, ill-paid and just about as boring as watching jello set in a cracked bowl.

The whole place bobbed and floated on huge cedar logs held together with mammoth lengths of boom chain. Even when the wind was slight and the water calm, every square inch of the jeezless hole rocked and wobbled. When the storms whipped down the inlet you could get sick to your stomach just sitting on a chair trying to read a magazine. The cedar logs were covered with rough-sawn random-width planks gone silver-grey in the sun and sea water. A tourist, seeing it all for the first time, especially on a clear day, would think it beautiful. Living there, especially when rain and spray made the bleached boards as slippery as fish guts spilled on a rock, a body would think it half a step removed from hell. Unless you happened to be a salmonbelly and something inside you thrummed when you smelled low tide or saw a shaggy feathered heron lumbering into the sky like some kind of prehistoric flying reptile.

Rowan loved it. She stepped off the company boat with a pack on her back and a big suitcase dangling from each hand, and the first whiff of diesel mixed with raw cedar and fresh-cut fir hit her nostrils like a homecoming welcome. The September wind had an edge to it that made her shiver, but not with cold as much as excitement and recognition. The ripe stench of low tide and the greasy tang of outboard fuel tickled her just behind the belly button. She stepped out of everyone else's way and just stood, weighed down by her few earthly possessions, staring around her with wide eyes, grinning happily.

"Come on, kiddo," Mary grunted, muling her own gear down the float. "Let's us go find out where they've put us."

If it had been hauled up on the beach, set on foundations, levelled and squared away properly, it would have been a cottage. But there was no beach to set it on. High tide ended and the steep slope began, thrusting up until a mountain goat would have surrendered rather than try to remain upright.

"You mean it all just goes into the chuck?"

"That's it, kiddo."

"Just right straight into the underneath of the float? And then people catch fish off the float and eat them? Or crabs or . . ."

"Hey, Smoocherooni, what's the difference? You flush a toilet in town and it all goes wisher-washin' down a maze of pipes and into the sea, or you flush the jane here and it goes into the sea without the bother of all that piping, so what's the diff?"

"I didn't know," Rowan admitted. "And now I do."

"Well, there you have it. That's why they say ignorance is bliss."

"Yeah. So it's folly to be wise, right?"

"You got'er, kiddo."

"I guess . . ." Rowan stared at the porcelain bowl set over a hole in the floor. "I always thought you pulled the flush and it all went . . . away."

"Darlin'," Mary put her arm around her granddaughter and gave a short, hard squeeze, "there is no Away."

Three bedrooms and a big all-purpose kitchen-dining room-living room-wotzit. A small stove for both heat and cooking, with a plumber's nightmare of piping in the firebox to heat the water in the big metal tank behind the stove. An old lightweight copper tub in the bathroom, and, of course, the toilet and a small basin. Sometimes, sitting on the jane, Rowan could hear the waves slapping on the other end of the short pipe and in rough weather you might even get a cold splash on your butt.

The floor was always chilly, in spite of the triple-plank flooring. The previous occupant had nailed gunny sacking tight over the planks, then put down linoleum, tacked around the edges and held in place with screwed-down brass stripping. Even so, you soon learned to wear a pair of grey wool socks over your cotton ones.

"We'll get some of those braided rugs from the catalogue," Mary promised. "They help keep the draughts at bay."

"This isn't a bay," Rowan laughed, "it's an inlet." She pulled her feet up and sat cross-legged on the chair, like a babba-yoga of some kind. "It's pretty bare," she decided. "Kind of . . . kind of like a schoolroom when there's nobody in it."

"Yeah, well, we'll fix 'er up and make a home out of it."

"Sure we will."

They smiled determinedly at each other.

And they did just that. They sat at the table with the Wish Book and looked at things like linoleum and braided rugs. "Linoleum'd be a bitch to get shipped in," Mary sighed, "and once it's here, there's the trying to get it laid down properly. But maybe we can manage. Never know till you try, I suppose. Just don't get carried away on colours, you can get awful sick and tired of bright red with orange and green squares!"

"All the plain stuff costs more," Rowan observed. "If it's ugly, it doesn't cost much. That's odd. I mean you have to make the stuff, whatever it is. So you have to do that much. Then you start adding colour and that prob'ly costs, I mean you'd think putting one colour wouldn't cost as much as putting two or three or four or five. So the ones with all the colours ought to cost more, and they don't."

"It's the price you pay for being poor," Mary grumbled, rolling herself a cigarette. "That's so when the government census taker walks in the house he knows right away if you're high-tone or hog-feet. Only rich people can afford to buy stuff that's quiet and doesn't scream 'catalogue, catalogue, catalogue'."

Mary was out of bed long before the sky began to lighten. She turned up the flow of oil to the stove, so the place would be halfway warm when the kid wakened, then she dressed in the chilly kitchen and pulled on her drybacks and gumboots. She walked the length of the slick float to the cook house and went in to start making breakfast for the single guys who lived in the bunkhouses. While the coffee was perking and the bacon and sausages crisping, she packed lunches until she was sick of the sight of sliced bread, cheese, mystery meat, mayonnaise, peeled hard-boiled eggs and huge slices of pie.

She had time for two cups of coffee and a couple of rollies before the first of the starving arrived. They came in quietly, and they left their gumboots in the hall room with their drybacks, pulled slippers from the back pockets of their redstrap jeans and walked clean-footed into the cook shack. Not one of them would have dared track mud on Mary's floor. Not because they were afraid of Mary, but because the others would never have tolerated such low-rent behaviour. They goddamn ate in this place, okay, and even a pig won't muck up the corner where he eats. Whatsa matter, you born in a goddamn barn or something? Jesus Christ, I might have to work in mud and shit but I don't have to sit and eat in it.

They ate as if they wouldn't see food again for a month, then picked up their lunch kits, filled their stainless steel thermoses from the enormous coffee urns, doctored the brew to suit individual taste, and left quietly, each of them thanking Mary, each of them telling her "good breakfast, Mare, thanks." They knew they were lucky. Mary could have taken ditch rat, rolled it in flour, tossed in some salt and pepper and Greek spices, cooked it in a rusty tin can over an open fire and made it seem like something you'd pay good money for in a restaurant. And she made plenty, too.

She had all those dishes to wash, tables to scrub, sugar and salt and pepper shakers to clean and refill. She had bread to bake, buns to bake, cakes, cookies and pies to make and bake. Potatoes by the sack to peel, meat by the mountain to season and cook. One thing after another, one job after another, with a couple of hours off in the afternoon to put her feet up and have a bit of a rest. It was steady, but it wasn't unreasonable or back-breaking, and there were satisfactions to it. The kid showed up for lunch and they ate together at the table in the kitchen, surrounded by good smells and stacks of cooling baked goods. No more Krap Dinner, no more noodle-in-a-mug pretend soup. She filled the kid with pork chops and beef steak, with cold roast and hash browns, and she sent her home with an apple pie or a stack of butter tarts.

Rowan took her correspondence course to the big room where the single guys could watch television after work, and sat with the dozen or so other kids reading the bullshit the government mailed out, then filling in the answers to the dumbdick questions. If she got stuck, which didn't happen often, there was a mother or a big sister or an older brother to help out, and at least you weren't trapped there all day. Once your section was done, it was done, and you could take off and find interesting things to do.

At first she fished off the float, but all you really got there was rock cod or tommy cod or flounder, and she couldn't get past the knowledge the damn things had probably fed on what flushed out of the float houses. Similarly, there was something off-putting about emptying a crab trap and knowing the big green-backed monsters had grown up feasting on unmentionables.

"No different than what most people catch," Mary insisted.

"Yeah, but . . ."

"So why not teach yourself to row? Long's you wear a floater jacket I'm not gonna pitch fits about you bein' out on the chuck. You weren't born to drown, kiddo, or you'd'a already done 'er in the bathtub."

"Would it be safe?"

"Safe? What's safe? You could trip on a shoelace and fall head first against the oil stove, crack your skull, wind up spastic. You could fall outta bed and bust your neck. Nothin' is *safe*, darlin'. But if you wear your floater and don't try to do what you're not ready to do, you're prob'ly as safe in a rowboat as you are sittin' on the jane. If you never do anythin', you'll never *do* anythin'. And if you're bored, it's up to nobody else but you to do somethin' about that. After all, if you hadn't already been doin' new stuff, some of it not very safe at all, you'd be lyin' in bed wearin' a diaper and drinkin' your meals out of a bottle with a rubber nipple. Most dangerous thing you'll ever encounter, you've already done. Bein' born."

The boat was small, and it took some practice before she could get it to do anything but go in circles, and most winter days were too rough for her to go very far anyway, but by the time the spring storms had blown themselves out she was confident enough to head off right after lessons and get herself away from the toilets. She rowed around the headland to the next bay and dropped her line over the side, jigging for cod or pretending she was trolling for salmon. She didn't catch salmon, she knew you needed a trolling motor to do that, and at first she turned the dogfish loose when she hooked one.

"Why?" Mary laughed. "In England they call them rock salmon and sell 'em in fish'n'chip shops. You just whap off the tail and let 'em drain over the side and they're good to eat. Try it, I dare you."

"The one time I kept one it stank like stale piss."

"Because you didn't drain out the blood. They got ammonia or something in their blood. You drain that out and they're better'n cod. No bones to choke on, just this spine thing up the middle."

"You gotta be kiddin'," one of the loggers blurted. "Damn things aren't good for anything except maybe crab or prawn bait! I wouldn't eat bloody dogfish on a bet."

"You think not, eh?" Mary laughed. He stared at her and let it all drop, suddenly very aware of boneless fish fillets. The gyppo owner just smiled to himself. Every bit of free food he could get into the workies was a bonus, and if Mary didn't mind cooking it, and the kid didn't mind catching it, maybe they'd make enough over costs to justify living like outcasts from what most thought of as real life. Might even be worth his while to give the kid a couple of dollars now and again to keep her interested.

Rowan took traps from the pile against the outboard shed and set them off the rocks, with little packages of raw meat trimmings for bait. She saved fish heads for crab bait, and tails, too, and there was never any trouble about selling what she hauled out of her traps. If Mary didn't want it for crab salad for the crew, some wife would be happy to buy a few for supper.

As long as she was back in the cook shack in time to sit down to a big plate of food in the kitchen before Mary had finished the supper dishes, Rowan's time was her own. Some days she headed out in the rowboat and did no more than set a couple of crab traps, then lean back against the seat, her butt on a spare life jacket, a book propped on her knees. Some days she landed the rowboat and prowled the rocky beach or tried to get close to the huge snags where the bald eagles nested; you could find great eagle feathers at the foot of the snags and there was always the chance the eagle would crap on you and give you seven years' good luck.

One day she watched as an eagle tried to boot a heron out of a small bay. The heron didn't seem the least bit interested in fighting, she just flew from her jumble-of-sticks nest at the top of a snag and down to the mud flats. There she stood ankle-deep, waiting, still as still could be; then faster than your eye could follow, the big jabby-beak would dip, then lift, and heron would swallow and take her waiting position again. And all the while the eagle circled, cackling and screeching insults.

When the heron took to the sky, the eagle started dive bombing, and each time, just before the enraged eagle slammed into her, heron dipped one wing and slid out of the way. Finally, her patience worn thin, heron let loose one loud *grooonk* of warning. Eagle took it as a challenge and flew up, up, up until all Rowan could see was a wavery speck. Then eagle dove, legs down and stiff, intent on ripping heron to shreds and claiming the entire bay. Just before eagle struck, heron rolled on her back and spread her wings, cupping as much air as she could hold, then she slammed her wings together with a noise almost exactly like the one you get by blowing up a brown paper bag, then bursting it with your hand.

Heron rolled back right side up, and eagle, caught by the burst of air and sound, wobbled in flight, dazed and groggy. Rowan laughed, and her imagination re-drew what her eyes actually saw. She pictured the eagle with a bent beak, crumpled feathers, and eyes rolling in circles. Heron gronked answer to the laughter, returned to her tangled jumble of sticks and settled herself as calm as if nothing at all had happened.

A heron feather drifted down from the sky, and Rowan caught it before it landed. She took it to correspondence class with her and told about the encounter and how heron had won. The big sister running the class that day showed Rowan how to bead the shaft of the feather, and told her it was especially lucky to get a feather that came from a live bird, and get it before it touched anything else. "All the power," she smiled, "comes with it, from the bird, directly to you. It's very special." Rowan felt so good about that, she didn't even mind having to be in school to learn about it. She worked carefully and patiently, and when her feather was done she hung it above her bed, so the power would be over her while she slept.

III

The poker game had been going on for years. Nobody had the slightest idea how many zillions of dollars had been slid across the table top in ones, twos, fives, tens, twenties. The supper stuff was no sooner cleaned up and put away, than the first faded denim butt was sliding onto the chrome-legged chair, the first calloused hands were reaching for the Copenhagen can or rolling a smoke, patiently waiting for the other players to arrive. Some sipped beer or wine, some nipped at pocket flasks, one or two walked outside to inhale some Indica, and a few stuck to tea or coffee. Faces changed, voices changed, but the game just went on, as endless as the tide.

Mary ignored the game for the first ten months. She had clear memories of money lost and money won at oilcloth-covered tables; the winning was great, the losing wasn't. She told herself time and time again she had to keep her nose clean this time, she had Rowan to consider, she'd made enough mistakes with Carol, no need to make the same mistakes this go-round.

It was boredom did it. Boredom and loneliness. She tried to make friends with the few other women in camp, but it didn't work out for her, or for them. They were married and she wasn't. Period. They were pleasant enough, but not one of them was able to believe every single woman in the world didn't have her sights set on stealing their particular old man. And by the time Mary was finished working, they were well into their own family routines, bath time, story time, bedtime for the kids, then an hour or so of conversation or silence with the better half before going to bed to rest up for another day of the same. The afternoon break Mary welcomed gratefully hit at just the time the other women were most occupied with domestic concerns. And as much as Mary loved Rowan, there are built-in limits to the kind of conversation you can have with a kid, however much you love her.

And once that kid has gone to bed, there you are, sitting in a float house, too keyed up to go to sleep, staring at a pile of novels, feeling as if you will screech if you have to read one more chapter of a story about people whose lives have nothing to do with your own. And yes, there was a satellite dish, but what good does that do when everything that comes from the television assumes that anything interesting, entertaining or worthwhile happens in cities thousands of miles from what you know as reality?

So, finally, one night, Mary turned up with some money in her pocket, her can of tobacco and her packet of Zig Zag blue papers, and sat in on the game. Just an hour or two, she told herself, just enough to unwind a bit and pass some time.

It didn't help her reputation, what was left of it, and it didn't do anything at all to weld a connection between her and the other women in camp. It unwound her, sure, and it passed time, sure, but it did more than either of those things. And she knew it.

She cared, at first. She didn't let anyone know she cared, but she cared. She stopped caring the night all hell bust loose down the far end of the float houses.

Nobody on the coast will openly admit to being racist. There's always a supposedly good reason for hating whoever the latest underdog is. After all, everyone knows Eyeties will talk about you behind your back in that jabber they call a language, and everyone knows Polacks might be good workers but can't learn anything new. There's no denying Scandihoovians are just about the best loggers and finest neighbours a person could want but they are clannish and they do stick together something awful. Jews, well, they don't work in the bush, they can't survive out of cities, but they do well there because they stick together even more than the Scandihoovians do and every Jew child, it's a well-known fact, gets three chances to go into business for her-or-himself. They get financed by the other Jews and if they go tits-up the first time, well, so what, they get financed again, and if they go tits-up the second time, well, maybe they should be sent off to business administration school, and if they go tits-up the third time, that's it, go to work for someone else. But the rug-riders, well, what does anyone know about them? They stick together like cat shit to a new wool blanket, you have to take them to one side and explain to them about socks or they'll walk around in a four-hundred-dollar suit, white shirt, tie, and eighty-dollar leather oxfords with their bare ankles poking out for all the world to see. They eat funny, and there's no denying that, and nobody in their right mind would move into a house after those people have lived in it because the reek of their cooking gets right into the walls and you can't get rid of it no matter what you do. The men will smile at you and all the time be planning how to screw you out of something and the buggers are going to ruin insurance rates because once they found out about insurance they all started setting their houses on fire and driving their new cars for two and a half years then arranging with a friend to have the car stolen and wrecked so they can use the settlement money to buy another new one. They go to the feed store and buy a big sack of crushed corn meal and another sack of ground buckwheat, and they live on pancakes with bits of goat meat wrapped inside. They don't even know that stuff from the feed store is full of chemicals and only good for animals, no, and there's no telling them, either. The men are all chasing white women but don't let a white man look at one of their women or the swords and knives'll come out and every time you pick up the paper there's another one of them arrested for immigration violations, sneaking in on someone else's identification or something. And likely as not you'll also read about them fighting and ripping each other's guts out with punji sticks for Chrissakes. Want to know how many of them live in a house, well count the windows and multiply by thirty-two and that'll give you some idea. And no use trying to be friends with them because they don't know what friendship is and anyway behind all that smiling and nodding the buggers have contempt for everything about this country except the money they can make. But racism? Oh hell, that's what they have down in the States, and it's a cryin' shame when you think about it, especially the way they treat their blacks, because how many people do you know who could sing and dance the way all the black people can. Racism? Well no, it isn't anything like that at all, it's just tellin' the truth the way it is.

Two houses side-by-each had rug-rider families living in them. The kids took their correspondence courses with the other kids and except for some vocabulary problems, things worked out fine. The men worked hard, the three women helped each other and the babies were cute as bug's ears. But what's going on there, anyway, two houses, four men, three women, and kids back and forth between the places until you don't know which belongs to which and do you figure they share that third woman, or what?

Mary had just won forty-three dollars when the uproar started. She was never sure exactly what happened, or in what order. One minute she was picking money off the oilcloth and the next everyone was yelling and shouting. She followed the crowd out onto the floats, and stood, suddenly sick to her stomach, staring at the bright orange and red glare.

She ran, then. Terrified the flames would race along the cedar shingled roofs, and set her own float shack afire with Smoocherooni still inside, she just started pumping her arms and legs, plowing through the shocked crowd, feet hammering on the planking, down the float to the front door, through the door and into the back bedroom where Rowan was just starting to wake up. Mary grabbed Rowan by the arms, pulled her upright, and raced back out the door with her, not even waiting long enough for the kid to shove her feet into sneakers or slippers.

By then men were running with the canvas and rubber hose, someone was starting up the generator, someone else plugging in the pump, and miraculously, everyone seemed to know exactly what to do.

Rowan broke loose and raced toward the fire screeching wildly, and vanished into the thick smoke. Mary screamed until she thought her throat would burst, and then Rowan was coming out of the smoke, hauling two little kids behind her, pushing them off the float into the chuck and dragging them back out again, dripping wet. Mary raced forward to grab Rowan and instead found herself hoisting the four-year-olds on her hips and thundering away from the flames. The little kids just stared, eyes as big as saucers, not even crying, shaking with cold and shock.

One of the women lived an hour or more, her skin charred, her hair gone, the melted material of her sari embedded in the blisters and raw open cracks of her flesh. They did what they could but all the experts in the world couldn't have saved her. The others fried. Men, women, kids, the whole lot of them except for the two Rowan had managed to get to safety.

The seaplane arrived two hours past dawn and the RCMP walked around taking pictures and writing notes. An hour later, the seaplane took off again, and the two stunned and wide-eyed kids flew off in their pyjamas.

"What's going to happen to them?" Rowan asked.

"Either they'll go to live with relatives," Mary answered, "or they'll go to foster homes, I guess."

"But not here, huh? Not here where they know everybody."

"Nobody here knows everybody, honey. We're all next best to strangers to each other. Besides. . . they aren't our kind of people."

"You told me we were all the same." Rowan's eyes filled with tears. "You said beauty was only skin deep and after that we were all just meat, bones, and guts."

"That's true," Mary said firmly, "but there are different languages and ways of doing things, all the same."

Rowan nodded, even though she didn't understand or agree. She walked over to the little rowboat, got in and pulled on the oars, her back to the charred ruin of what had been two adjacent float houses. The smell lingered on the breeze, acrid and stinging, but that wasn't what made the tears slide from her eyes and down her face. Someone ought to have said, "Oh, they'll be fine with us, we'll just set up another bed, what's one or two more, and at least they know people." But nobody had. And somehow, though she didn't understand why, she hadn't dared ask Mary to be the one to make the offer. She didn't want to be disappointed when Mary said no.

She wakened that night and lay in the darkness. knowing Mary was just a loud yell away, knowing there was nothing lurking in the closet, nothing crouched under the bed, nothing waiting in the corner of the room. She knew all she had to do was jump out of bed, run across the floor to the front door and along the mist-slick float to where Mary was sitting in on the card game. She knew she didn't even really have to run at all, just start hollering. But it felt lonely, all the same. It felt as if in all the world there was just her and her grandmother. And that didn't feel right. It seemed to her a body ought to know there were lots of others ready to step up and put an arm around a person's shoulders, smile down and say It's okay, Sweetheart. She wondered if there had ever been a time or place when things were done that way. She rolled onto her side, staring at the darker blur of the wall. She wanted to cry, but it seemed a silly waste of time if there was nobody to hear or care. Yes, she could call out and Mary would come, and then what? What words would explain the overwhelming sense of loss and loneliness? After all, what had she lost, it wasn't her house burned, it wasn't her people burned, it wasn't her flying off to a big black scary future, why did the memory of the departing float plane fill her with such terror and such hollow grief?

Mary couldn't have explained to anybody, not even herself, what it was had changed for her after the fire. Whatever it was, she gave up wasting any time at all worrying what people might think of her. If the wives wanted to think she was humpin' herself to a fare-thee-well with all the single guys, let 'em. About time they thought about something, and if they were talking about her, they weren't talking about her friends. And if she had a drink or two, or three or four during the poker session, what harm was she doing anybody, Christ almighty, you're a long time dead and you don't laugh once rigor mortis has set in.

They didn't live full-time in the float camp. When the bush was closed for fire season, most of them gypsied off, taking the freight ferry out and catching a bus to wherever they could rent or lease a car, van or motor home and drive off to visit relatives or go on holiday like normal people. Rowan and Mary usually checked in to a motel or auto court and sacked out there, catching up on movies and shopping for new jeans and new high-top Nike basketball sneakers. When the rains started and it was safe to go back into the bush, they did the trip in reverse. During snow shutdown, they headed out again, correspondence course tucked in a box, and they celebrated more than one Christmas in a motel unit, with a chicken instead of a turkey, because, after all, there were only the two of them and anyway the oven was too small for a big bird.

They lived in camps in Frohlander Bay, in Clamshell Bay, and at Tarbox Point, they lived in Mid-Point and Galleon and Downrigger, they lived in Esperance and in Calm Harbour and once they lived two miles down the beach from where someone at some time had set up an enormous still and made rotgut to smuggle below the forty-ninth during prohibition. Rowan couldn't believe the size of the metal vats or the miles of copper piping coiled up like vertigris'ed guts. It took no time at all for the bunkhouse boys to figure out a way to salvage various bits and pieces and set up their own smaller version, then swipe a twenty-pound sack of rice, a big package of raisins and a ten-pound sack of sugar from the cookhouse. Actually, Rowan wondered if any of it had really been swiped or if Mary was in on the whole thing from the start. Certainly she sipped her share of the rocket fuel once it started to drip from the condenser. "Oh, it's well aged," she said solemnly, "I bet it's at least four hours old. A body has to do something to poison the intestinal parasites."

Rowan found her own schedules and routines. If she was lonely she didn't know it, she'd spent most of her life not knowing there was any other way to be, and you don't miss what you never knew. When the rain pelted down and the wind howled like a bitch in heat she just lost herself in the correspondence courses and did lesson after lesson for lack of any other options. When the weather was kind, the lessons sat in the cardboard box.

Mary didn't push one way or the other. "It's your life, kiddo," she said, lighting another cigarette. "If you don't give a shit, there aren't many others who will. One way or the other, sooner or later, you've gotta get 'em done."

"I know." Rowan sandpapered the handgrips of her oars carefully, the fine sawdust landing on a piece of newspaper on the floor. "I've got them done. If I mail 'em all off at the same time, they're apt to say something in Victoria. So I just mail off a few every week."

"But they're done?"

"Yeah."

"Why not mail 'em off and get new ones?"

"Then I'd have to do *them*, too," Rowan winked. "And they'd start to expect something."

The boss saw her rowing back with a gunnysack of cod and went to Mary to suggest the kid ought to be doing more than lallygagging around in a boat.

"She should either go to school or start working," he decided.

"Yeah?" Mary put down her rolling pin, sat on a chair, stuck a cigarette in her mouth and lit it. "I'm not sendin' her off to boarding school, and she's not workin' full time in this cook shack with me. What do you care?"

"She could get into trouble," he decided.

"You could get into trouble yourself," Mary cautioned. "Doesn't pay to poke your nose into the cook's business."

"A kid like that, with time on her hands and a bunkhouse fulla young randy guys, that's like gas and matches."

"Butt out," Mary said coldly. "She ain't got time on her hands, what she's got is callouses from rowin' out to the cod pools and back. And them randy young single guys ain't animals from another planet, they're all somebody else's kids."

"Easy, easy," he said, backing toward the door and wishing he'd never even come into the cook shack. "I was only thinkin'. . . ."

"Well, don't." She stubbed out her smoke, stood up and got ready to go back to her pie crust. "You ain't got enough practice thinkin' to do a good job of 'er."

That fire season, Rowan met a guy named Jerry Pritchard at the Collieries Dam Park, where she went most afternoons to swim and to lie in the sun, neither asleep nor awake but comfortably somewhere between the two. At first they just talked, then they pooled their lunches and shared sandwiches and pop.

"You like to go to the show tonight?" he asked.

"Sure," she said easily, "what's on?"

"I don't know," he laughed, his face pink. "I didn't even think about going until I started thinkin' about maybe going with you."

Mary just stared, then finally nodded, and Rowan hit the bathroom. She filled the tub and had a good soak, then a scrub. She washed her hair, put on her best jeans and was just finished brushing out her hair when Jerry arrived, as spiffed in his own way as Rowan was in hers. Mary watched them leave, then went to the cupboard under the sink where she kept the Ajax, the sudsy ammonia, the dish detergent and the big bottle of Gilbey's gin.

"Dear God," she said aloud, "this is me. Please don't let it start all over again, I didn't handle 'er the last time and I don't know as I could do any better this time." She was just about half packed when Rowan came home at midnight.

"Have a good time?" Mary asked carefully.

"It was great!" Rowan's skin was flushed and she was grinning from ear to ear. Something had changed forever. "I met a whole bunch of kids."

"Yeah? They nice?"

"Most of them. Different, but nice." Rowan looked at the nearly empty bottle and shook her head gently. "You better be careful," she warned, "you know some of those ice cubes are tainted."

"Yeah. You're right." Mary finished her drink and managed to focus her eyes. "Guess it's time for bed," she decided.

Maybe God heard. Or maybe Rowan just wasn't her mother. The thing with Jerry lasted until fire season ended, it even lasted two or three scrawled letters after Rowan and Mary went back to camp, but it had dribbled away before snow shutdown, and nobody's heart was even bent, let alone cracked or broken.

Jerry was followed by Sid, who was six feet tall and had thick blond hair and an older sister in nursing school, a sister whose ice skates fit Rowan's feet so Sid could teach her to skate. Mary worried her way through several bottles of gin that winter, but if she had reason to worry, Rowan didn't let her know what it was.

"Do you and I have to have any kind of discussion about birth control?" Mary asked. The silence stretched, then Rowan shook her head, her face as red as her woollen socks. "You're sure?" Mary probed.

Rowan got up from her chair, went into her bedroom and returned with a circular plastic disk. Mary looked at the little apricot-coloured pills ringed around it, one for each day.

"You figure they'll do you any good in the case?" she tried to tease, and knew it fell flat. "Nothin' is much use if you don't *use* it."

"I've been using these for almost two years," Rowan answered.

Mary nodded. She took a sip of her drink and lit another cigarette.

"I know there's a lot of hoo-rah about are they safe or not," Rowan continued, "but I figure number one, there's enough of us in this cabin already, and number two," she grinned, and Mary saw herself years earlier, spitting in the devil's eye, "it takes real intestinal fortitude to flirt with cancer."

"That's my kid."

Eventually Rowan Hanson's heart was broken, by a laughing second-loader who never intended to break her heart. She lay on her bed and wept stormy tears into her pillow, brooded for a week, then pulled up her socks and got on with life. Mary left her alone through the worst of it, but when Rowan was ready to pick up the pieces, Mary was ready, perhaps not wearing a cheerleader suit and waving pompons, but in her own way, totally on Rowan's team.

"So what I was thinking. . ." Mary poured coffee, adding a hair of the dog to her own. "We'll be in snow shutdown soon. Maybe this time we should try to live like people do. I mean, you don't want to spend the rest of your life bobbin' on the waves in some float shack you have to share with roof rats and squirrels, working as cook's helper in a logging camp. Young woman like you probably wants some kind of real job and real life. So maybe we should just pack 'er up and try to be Townies, what do you think?"

Rowan looked up from her coffee. Mary smiled, and Rowan felt wrapped in love. She saw for the first time the lines in Mary's face, the sagging skin under her grandmother's eyes, the years of hard work etched in the knobby knuckles of her fingers. Mary's fifty candles were blown out, but it had been one helluva good cake. They could have years more together, why not have them with hot running water, a mammoth bathtub, and a job that only chewed up eight hours of your day instead of fourteen.

"I'd like that," she nodded. "I was thinking I'd like to take that course they have on driving trucks. Maybe after a while I'd find a way to swing it so I had my own, then you could come with me. Might be the only way we get to travel much."

"Yeah," Mary smiled, even though she figured their chances of owning a truck were about the same as a snowball's chances in hell. "There's got to be more to life than this coast. Stands to reason it's gotta be tacked onto something else!"

They moved into town and took an apartment within walking distance of anywhere you'd want to go. Mary got a job before all their stuff was unpacked and in place, but it took Rowan another two months to find something full time. That taught her more than any number of lectures could have done, and she was determined to learn to do the kind of work people would pay her to do.

"Now that we're in town," Mary said, settling herself on the ten-dollar geriatric couch they had bought at the Used'n'Re-Used, "there'll be young studs sniffing around all the time. I never figured we needed to have much in the way of 'a talk' but. . . there's one thing I do want you to know."

"Yes, Grandmother dear," Rowan teased.

Mary grinned and took a bracing gulp of her overproof drink, then dove in headfirst. "People's gonna Expect you to do things a certain way and live your life by rules they never explain, they just lay 'em down and that's that. And you can do that if you want. Lots of people do that because they want to be what people Expect other people to be. But if any of that stuff sticks in your throat, just cough 'er up and spit 'er out. What I want for you might not be what other people think I should want. I want you to be able to live with yourself."

Mary took another good stiff gulp of her poison and stared down at the tabletop for long moments, sorting through her memories. Rowan sat listening and waiting, not feeling the least little bit as if her Gran was lecturing her or preaching to her.

"There's stuff about what went down between me'n your mom that I don't feel good about," Mary went on, "and there's nothing I can do to change any of it. There was nothing I could do at the time. I'd'a done 'er different if I'd'a been able to, darlin', but I wasn't much older then than you are now and nobody had done much about tellin' me the truth of things so I had to find out for myself. But even if I don't feel good about it, I can live with it because I know I mighta made mistakes, but I never meant to do harm."

"Gran . . . it's okay."

"Not for you to say it's okay, nor for me, either. It just is. And it can't be changed." Mary reached for her tobacco can and papers and rolled herself a smoke. Rowan waited while her grandmother lit up and inhaled. "What I feel damned good about is you, Smoocherooni." Mary smiled and wiped her eyes. "I never for one minute regretted havin' you in my life. We've had some rough times, but who doesn't, prob'ly even the Queen'a'England has days when she feels someone is shovellin' crap onto her head. I love you, and I like you, and I'm prouda you. So anyway," and she laughed briefly, "I'm runnin' on here like some kind of old fool. What I'm tryin' to say is I felt from the get-go that you were my chance. A body only gets one good kick at the can, kiddo, and if you miss, you've blown 'er. So when it's your turn to take your kick at the can, you do 'er because you'll hate yourself forever if you let it pass you by."

"I love you, Gran. I wouldn't change anything." Rowan kissed the air between them, then winked to lighten the mood. "What's that other thing you were going to tell me?"

"Everything and everybody's on a scale from one to ten," Mary lectured, not quite looking at Rowan, "and I want you to remember this: there's nothin' much wrong as I can see with goin' to pubs or bars and havin' a good time. But don't ever forget that come closin' time, all the twos look like tens."

IV

Rowan Hanson drove the SPCA van to the corner of Fourth and Spruce and parked in the driveway, under the spreading branches of a gnarled apple tree. The lawn was thick with fallen blossoms, the spring breeze pulled other petals from the thick clusters on the boughs, and she walked through a rain of scented white flakes to the back door of the cedar-sided house.

The man who answered her knock was probably at least as old as the apple tree. He wore a button-front cardigan with leather elbow patches over a soft checked flannel shirt, and his pants had at one time been part of a suit, the knees now baggy and worn shiny. He invited her inside and immediately started making a pot of tea. Rowan wanted to say no, to tell him she didn't really have time, but she couldn't brush him off. He deserved more from her, somehow, and maybe all she could give him was ten minutes, but she would feel cheapened if she denied him at least that much.

"I don't like strife with the neighbours," he apologized, pouring steaming tea into the cup in front of her. "And I tried, I really tried, Miss. Went over and talked to them at least a dozen times. First few times they just listened, next few times they argued, the last couple of times they were real nasty. Told me to go to hell." He sighed. "And it isn't just that the garden gives me a lot of good food." He shook his white-fringed head. "It's more than that. The garden is just about all I have to *do* these days."

"Besides which," she agreed, "when all is said and done, you've got your yard fenced, and it *is* your yard."

"I don't begrudge anybody a dog," he said, sitting down and pulling his cup closer. "I've had a good few of them myself. But a body has to take the responsibility seriously. If it needs exercise you take it where it can run and not bother other folks. I think, anyway."

She nodded, sipped her tea and waited, hearing the soft tick tock tick tock of the cuckoo clock on the kitchen wall. The old man sighed again, and looked as if there was more he wanted to say, but he didn't speak. The silence stretched past awkward to comfortable. Rowan drank her tea, then pushed her chair back and smiled. "I'll get the live trap myself," she told him, and he nodded, troubled and probably wishing he had never phoned.

"It's in the basement," he said softly. "The side door is unlocked. I feel bad about this, Miss," he blurted.

"I know." She almost patted his shoulder, but didn't. "I think you've been more than tolerant. I'm afraid I'd have blown the whistle months ago."

"Nearly did this last year." He walked with her to the back door. "Couldn't bring myself to do it, though. But then the other night, well, it was just too much. Dug big holes, tramped through everything, then went after my old cat. Didn't get her down out of the tree until past noon! And my bones are too brittle to be climbing up apple trees, believe me."

"No reason why you should have to. You take care of your cat, it's not up to you to take care of the neighbour's dog."

His relief showed in his faded eyes.

He waited on the porch while Rowan went down the side steps and through the door into the shadowed coolness of the basement. The live trap was right in front of the door, the lab-shepherd cross sitting in it whining eagerly. Rowan couldn't believe the old man had managed to get the cage and the dog down the steps and into the cellar all by his lonesome. The dog must weigh almost as much as the old guy himself.

She took the loop-ended leash from her pocket, opened the door of the cage and, as the dog rushed through, slipped the loop over its head and around its neck. It hit the end of the leash with a jerk, then tugged and yapped frantically. Obviously it had little experience with leash, or with collar for that matter. "Settle down," she warned. The dog lunged, its nails scrabbling on the cement floor, and Rowan tugged sharply.

She led the half-hysterical dog from the basement to the van, opened the back door, then reached inside and opened the holding cage. The dog didn't want to get in, but the choke-leash gave it few options. It went in, Rowan closed the door and that was that.

She went back to the basement for the live trap, closed the basement door and headed for the van. The old man watched, apologetic, and Rowan smiled at him. "It'll be all right," she assured him. "If you get any flak from them, let me know and I'll go see them."

"They aren't home from work until after six," the old man blurted, "and your place closes at five-thirty."

"Oh, that's okay," she grinned, "we expect to work overtime."

"They'd wait, you see," he told her, anger replacing his worry. "Wait until after supper, then let it off its chain to run loose. Poor brute spent hours every day trying to lunge off its chain and then all of a sudden it's off and racing like mad around the neighbourhood, half crazy if you ask me."

"You won't be bothered by this one again," she promised.

"You aren't going to kill it, are you?" he worried again.

"There's always someone wants a big dog," she lied, "and is willing to put some time into training it. People in the country, people on farms, we get them coming by all the time."

The old man wanted to believe that, so he did. He swallowed it hook, line and sinker. Rowan stored the live trap in the back of the van, closed the door and moved to the driver's seat. The old man stood on his back porch watching as she backed the van out of the driveway, turned onto the boulevard and then, checking her mirrors, eased out onto the street.

She could hear the dog whining and scratching in the back. "Settle down," she called easily. "Just settle down back there!" It didn't, and she reached out to turn on the radio. The music didn't settle the dog down, either. "Didn't anybody bother to teach you how to behave?" she asked. The dog barked, then tried to chew the metal bars of the cage. "Boy, you're sure not collecting many good points," she warned.

The dog fought the leash all the way from the van to the big kennel cage. Once in the kennel yard and free of the leash, it lunged repeatedly, trying to get through the mesh. Its gums bled from trying to gnaw the metal, and it became even more hysterical at the taste of its own blood.

Rowan went into the office and took off her jacket, then sat at the desk filling out the report. Glenda was working the phone, which rang as soon as she hung up from each conversation. To keep her notes up to snuff, she had to let it ring half a dozen times before answering again. The sound of the phone made all the dogs in the kennel bark and yap senselessly, and Rowan had to concentrate on ignoring their noise.

She worked at her desk until well past six. Glenda went home at five-thirty, leaving the answering machine to handle the phone calls. The dogs calmed down without the constant ringing, and a kind of uneasy peace wrapped the place.

Rowan went out to the kennels and checked the date tags. The dogs were supposed to have three days' grace from the time they were picked up, but nobody did anything until at least two weeks had passed. Either the owners came to claim them and pay the fines, or someone who wanted a dog showed up and adopted the good ones, the cute ones, the handsome ones.

What was left was not, for the most part, worth house room. Half wild, snarling, obviously mean; or trembling, cowed, and broken in spirit. She took the losers one at a time to the cement shed, then placed each in the big metal box. All you had to do was close the lid of the box and contact was made. That meant that in the time it took to go back for another loser, the one in the box was being electrocuted.

She removed dog number one, dead now, and lifted dog number two into the box. She closed the lid and went for dog number three. Dog after dog until number sixteen was lifted from the box and laid with the others in the incinerator. Rowan sighed, turned on the switch and winced at the *whoof* as the propane ignited. She checked the kennels, cleaned some mess from a couple of the yards, made sure the survivors were set for the night, then went back to the office. The incinerator would be finished in another hour and she had plenty of time to get to the bottom of her desk work. The answering machine tape would record the messages: dogs roaming at large, dogs biting children, dogs chasing cats, dogs overturning garbage.

The SPCA has found the following animals. These descriptions are general only. Please state pet number.

DOGS:

#124 Fem. Husky X, black, tan and white, black nylon collar with clasp, adult, 500 block 10th St.

#125 Neut. male Puli, black, adult, 700 block Ash

#126 Fem. Shepherd, black, tan & white, recent mom, adult, 600 block Skeena

#127 Male Retriever X tan with grey face, choke chain, adult, corner Strickland and Kennedy

#128 Fem. jack russel terrier, white, black patches, brown ears, adult, 5th and Bruce

#129 Male pit bull, black-brown brindle, adult, no collar, face scarred

#130 Rottweiler, male, black/tan adult, brown collar, tattooed

#131 Dcsh'nd black, white face, leather collar

#132 Maltese-poodle cross female, pregnant, white, fuzzy very friendly

#133 Female boxer, beige, white chest, black mask, ears trimmed, tattoo inner flank

CATS:

#256 Calico female

#257 Orange tabby female

#258 Black-white tom

#259 Neutered male silver tabby

She was in the cement shed, turning off the propane and raking the ash from the incinerator, when the big Chrysler Imperial stopped in the gravel driveway. Rowan could easily have opened the door and stepped out to speak to the people, but she was officially off-duty now, and had been for almost an hour. She watched as the blond in the grey suit led the docile golden lab to the kennel fence and tied the chain to a metal post. Every male dog in the kennel immediately started barking, lunging against the fence, scratching at the cement flooring.

The man went back to the Chrysler, got in and drove off quickly. Rowan watched, then sighed deeply. She would bet ten dollars against the hole in any stale donut the dog tag had been removed from the collar. The bugger could have come during office hours. He could have arranged to have the dog boarded until a replacement home was found. Instead, he just left her tied to the post, a young bitch obviously in season, as good as guaranteed to wind up in the ash pit.

She locked the shed and walked toward the young lab. The bitch watched her suspiciously then stood, tail wagging slowly. "Hey, Babe," Rowan said, offering her hand. The bitch sniffed, then sat and lifted one paw. "Hey," Rowan laughed softly, "someone taught you shake-a-paw! Good girl." She hunkered, and stroked the dog's soft-eared head. The bitch did not lick her hand, did not roll onto her side and present her belly in submission, but she did lean against the stroking hand and make soft noises deep in her throat.

"Good girl," Rowan praised. She stood and the dog stood with her. "Someone paid big money for you. What happened, did you get out of the yard and have a romance with some mutt? You got a belly full of pups they'll never be able to sell? Dumb move, Babe."

She untied the chain and started toward the door of an empty kennel. The young bitch fell into place, heeling obediently. Rowan paused, one hand on the cage door. The dog stared up at her, then sat, waiting.

"Ah shit," Rowan sighed. The dog waited. Rowan took her hand from the kennel door and turned, and the dog rose to her feet and padded beside her, back to the office.

Rowan dropped the leash and the dog sat, watching as Rowan hauled out her wallet and pulled money from it. She put the money in the metal box, filled out the licence form, took a tag, registered the number stamped on it and fastened the tag to the dog's collar. "Okay," she said, stroking the soft golden ears, "Okay, Babe, you're legal. Let's go, we've got things to do before suppertime."

She locked up and walked with Babe to her car. "Into the back seat, Babe." She opened the car door and the dog jumped in and sat on the floor, her head above the level of the window. "We'll get you a bit of blanket or something as soon as we can," she promised.

Rowan drove away, and Babe sat on the floor, watching out the window, as calm as if she had spent her life in this particular car with this particular woman. "Not keeping a single one of those pups," Rowan warned. "Not a single solitary one of them. And then, by God, as soon as possible, it's spay-time in the swamp for you!"

She left Babe in the car when she went in to see Mary. The place might be called something else but it still smelled like a hospital. Mary was in bed, with the chrome crib-sides in place and the head of the bed cranked to sitting position. Fluid still dripped from the plastic bag down to the big bruised patch in her inner elbow.

"Hey, Gran." Rowan kissed the hot dry skin of Mary's cheek. "You eat your supper tonight?"

"Hey, darlin'," Mary wheezed, "tell me I never in my life cooked swill like what they cook here."

"You never did," Rowan vowed. "Whatever it was you cooked, it wasn't swill. Mystery meat, maybe, or dogfish instead of cod, but never swill. Want me to go get you something to eat?"

"I'm so hungry," Mary's eyes filled with tears, "I could eat a horse and chase down the rider. But what they're giving me isn't fit for man or beast."

"What do you want?"

"I'd give my soul to the devil for hot peppered chicken," Mary managed. "I keep tryin' to tell 'em it's my lungs has gone to hell, not my stomach, but they just keep on bringin' this stuff with no taste and no texture. And if I have to look at grey peas much more, I'll die just to get away from the sight!" Her voice trembled with something more than physical weakness. "I know four out of five people in the world go to bed hungry at night, and I know there's lots would just pack away this fuckin' swill, but I can't do 'er, darlin', I just can't do 'er."

"And no reason you should," Rowan agreed. "You've cooked enough good meals for other people you should be entitled to have a few good ones cooked for you!"

Half an hour later Mary was chewing slowly, the lines in her face softened, her breathing easier. "Ah, it's good," she sighed. She swallowed carefully but then coughed harshly anyway. "You're a wonder. Best thing I ever did for myself," she managed, "was go collect you from them."

"Best thing you ever did for me," Rowan corrected, chop-sticking food from the cardboard take-out container to her mouth.

Mary sipped her green tea, then picked another piece of chicken from her container with her shaking, nicotine-stained fingers. "I worry," she confessed, "about. . . after. I don't want no holyroller mealymouth putting me in a hole in the ground and then praying two-faced prayers over me."

"Maybe I can take you to work with me," Rowan forced herself to tease and grin, "toss you in the incinerator-oven with a coupla cats, then take the ashes home in a Mason jar and store you in with the towels and facecloths."

"Don't want to be stored," Mary shook her head. "It's that kind of thing gives me the pip! Embalming bodies as if they were something to be preserved for all time! Puttin'em in graveyards, using some of the best food-growing land in the world to store the dead, covering the grass up with headstones and statues, paying a fortune to mark some grave, as if every corpse was a saint and not something nobody even bothered to remember any more. People spend a goddamn fortune after dear old Granny has croaked, maybe they're trying to get folks to forget they had her locked away in a home for fifteen years before she drew her last breath. It's all too much for me to understand." She stopped talking, her breath coming in painful gasps. Rowan reached for the oxygen mask and held it over Mary's mouth and nose.

The withered woman sucked desperately, the dark colour faded from her lips, and finally she nodded. Rowan removed the mask, hung it on its hook again, turned off the flow of oxygen and continued eating as if nothing had happened. "Smother myself in a flow of words," Mary puffed. "Well, I don't care. Just don't spend a fortune on stupidity. Take me out on a herring scow and dump the ashes into the chuck. Save the Mason jar," she grinned wickedly, "you might want to preserve peaches or something."

"When I leave tonight," Rowan spoke carefully, "you watch out your window. Got something out there to show you." She put her container aside, and Mary handed over her own. Rowan closed the lids, then went for a warm wet facecloth and washed her grandmother's hands and face.

"You gonna tell me?" Mary demanded.

"A dog." Rowan dried Mary gently with a white towel. "Got me a

dog. Golden lab bitch. Probably purebred but I'll never get the papers."
She told Mary about the Chrysler Imperial and the blond in the grey
suit. "Make a person mad if she let herself get sucked into it," she
confessed. "They want the kids to experience the mystery of life or some
damn thing, then when it all gets to be just too much bother, they
dump 'em off after hours, without the licence tag so there's no way they
can be found out. For thirty dollars they could guarantee the dog will
be adopted, but by then the mystery and magic and miracle is just a
pain in the ass and they won't spend two cents more."

"Good dog?"

"I think so." Rowan stood, leaned over and kissed Mary's jaundiced
cheek. "She can shake hands. Heels. Sits and waits like she's supposed
to. Doesn't grovel."

"I hate a dog that grovels," Mary agreed. She patted Rowan's face
and for a minute they both blinked rapidly. "Sure do love you,
Smoocherooni."

"Love you, too, Smoocherooni-your-own-self."

Every night Rowan went for something nice for Mary's supper and
pretended not to notice how little her grandmother ate. Rowan also
pretended she didn't know the few bites Mary managed to pack away
to please Rowan were the only bites she managed to swallow all day.
Whatever it was that had turned her lungs to a death sentence was
growing up her throat, making swallowing increasingly difficult and
painful. But they both behaved as if all Mary had was some new form
of a chest cold. And about the time Mary began to really need the
oxygen hissing in the face mask, Rowan left, without any prolonged
farewells, without ever using the word goodbye, as if all she was doing
was stepping into the next room to refill the teapot or visit the facilities.

Rowan hated the smell in the not-hospital, hated the shiny floors,
hated the elevator and hated the need to go there. But they'd kept Mary
at home as long as they could, longer than was really good for either of
them, and there is a difference between scratching your head and
ripping out your hair. There were no points needed proving. When it
was time it was time, and they'd given in gracefully. But that didn't
have to mean either of them liked it that way.

Rowan opened the back door and snapped her fingers. "C'mon,
Babe."

The lab bitch came out of the car and stood, waiting for the next command. "Heel," Rowan suggested. She walked across the parking lot, the dog following. Rowan knew her grandmother was watching from the second floor window, and put on a show for her. "Sit, Babe." "Shake-a-paw, Babe." "Up, Babe." "Babe, go. Babe, stop. Babe sit. Come, Babe." The dog went through it all, eager to please. "Atta good Babe," Rowan praised. "Now, back into the car, that's it. Good girl, Babe." She waved, and though she couldn't see her grandmother, she knew Mary could see her. Rowan waved again, then climbed into her car and drove off, sniffing furiously, determined she would not, by God, cry where the old woman could see her. "No grovelling," she shouted, pounding her fist on the steering wheel. "Goddamnit, no grovelling or snivelling."

She knew Mary was back in bed with the mask over her mouth and nose, sucking desperately, and if the old biddy could be brave, so could the young one. But it was a kind of torment to know before you even reached for it that Mary's hand would either be hot and feverish or cold and clammy, the nails tinged blue, the skin dry and flaking. No matter how much good skin cream Rowan took up, no matter how much she rubbed on her grandmother's skin, it still looked like crepe, and it still felt thin enough to pull apart at the slightest touch.

She let Babe sniff around the small yard for fifteen minutes before taking her into the house and showing her the corner she was expected to make her own. "Home Sweet Home," Rowan said, spreading several old shirts from the rag bag on the linoleum. She patted the heap. Babe moved obediently, sat on the shirts and, on command, lay down, tail wagging gently.

"Hope you like leftover Chinese food." Rowan emptied the card-board containers into a large plastic bowl. She waited while the dog lay on the shirts, staring eagerly. "Come," Rowan remembered to say, the dog was up and across the kitchen, nose twitching eagerly. "You can probably drink out of the toilet bowl. It's clean. You'll find it on your own if you get thirsty."

She checked to be sure she had clean slacks and shirt for work the next day, then ran a tub of hot water and sat steaming away her tension and trying hard not to think about what the gurgle in Mary's chest meant. Too easy to blame cigarettes or even the manufacturers of cigarettes. Too easy, even, to blame the governments which for years happily collected massive taxes on cigarettes. She knew if Mary hadn't been able to buy tobacco and papers, she'd have grown her own leaves and rolled them in catalogue pages. She also knew it wasn't a streak of self-destructiveness or addictive personality behaviour. Of a million ways to die, it's at least sociable. "Oh, hell," Mary had said more than once, "give me a fuckin' break with all this non-smoker crap. Only last week they were primed to drop nuclear bombs to ensure world peace. What's in our food? Who poisoned the drinking water? How'd the damn hole get in the ozone layer? Spare me, please. If I'm killin' myself by smokin', at least I'm the one doin' it, not some bastard I never met nor voted for, neither."

It had started with a cough they thought was a cold, and treated with Benylin cough syrup. A bottle or two later and Mary switched to Benylin with codeine. Finally she went to the doctor. There were the usual pee-in-a-bottle contribute-blood-to-the-vampire tests, and a chest X-ray, which Mary told Rowan was just standard. "Hell," she shrugged, "they're determined to give you your dose of radiation, whether you want it or not."

They probably knew then, and told Mary, but she didn't tell Rowan. Months later, after she was in the hospital, the doctor said something about it all having been too far gone for surgery, chemo, or radiation, and Rowan was smart enough to put two and two together and come up with something between three and five. Mary just hadn't bothered spilling the bad news until it couldn't be hidden any longer. "Now don't get yourself in an uproar," she warned. "You know damn well I'm not the kind to volunteer to be a guinea pig. They want to experiment on someone they'll have to find someone else!"

Rowan didn't send all of Babe's pups to the electrocution cage, after all. She kept one to take Babe's milk, a dark-coated bitch with what looked like Doberman markings. As soon as the pup was weaned, Babe was at the vet's to be spayed. "You're next," Rowan promised the pup.

On days off and weekends she put the dog and her pup in the back seat, went to the not-hospital, got Mary dressed and into a wheelchair, took her down to the parking lot and transferred her to the front seat, then drove to some nice place where the dogs could play and Mary could sit, bundled as if it were winter, and watch the world she was preparing to leave. "That pup," she warned, "don't seem to know she should look before she leaps."

"Well, if she breaks her neck she'll die of it because I'm not putting good money into big vet bills on a mutt."

"Listen to you," Mary laughed, but the laugh turned to a cough that soon choked her. Rowan got the little oxygen bottle with the portable mask and waited until Mary had herself pulled together again. "You know full well you'd sell your socks if that's what it took," Mary teased. "You talk a tough line but you walk a soft one."

"Oh yeah, well, you'll see, that's all I got to say."

"If that's all you got to say, people'll get tired of listenin' to you talk. Be a bore bein' around someone who just says you wait and see you wait and see you wait and see," and they smiled at each other, understanding exactly what was really being said.

They phoned on a Thursday night, and Rowan went immediately to the not-hospital and accompanied Mary in the ambulance. She sat with her in the emergency ward, then walked beside the wheeled gurney to the elevator, and stood in the ascending cage holding her grandmother's fever-hot hand. "You gotta promise me," Mary breathed through the burble in her chest, "you gotta promise me you won't let yourself get all bust up about this."

"I promise," Rowan sobbed. "Is it okay if I just kind of crack for a while?"

"Hell," Mary struggled to smile, "we both been half cracked all our lives."

She sat beside Mary's bed, hearing her own heartbeat pounding in her ears like a drum beating softly, measuring time until it was over, then left, dry-eyed, and called a cab from the pay phone in the hallway. The cab took her back to the nursing home, where she got into her car and drove the soft pastel-dawn streets back to the small two-bedroom no-basement cottage. She parked the car, locked the doors and went into the house. The dogs met her, not leaping gleefully or barking happily, but nuzzling her hand, nudging her knee, watching her with big dark eyes. "Nothing coming down on you," she assured them.

Rowan made a pot of tea and sat in the big chair by the picture window, looking without seeing out at the little flower beds. Babe padded over and lay at Rowan's feet making soft grunting noises and pushing her damp nose against Rowan's ankle. "Butt out," Rowan sobbed, "it's got bugger-all to do with you." Babe sighed loudly and waited patiently. Rowan drank her tea and wiped her eyes, then reached for the phone to leave a message on the machine, telling them she wouldn't be in to work for a couple of days. Someone else could run the electrocution cage.

It was over, and more cleanly than she had dared pray it would be. Not a bad way to go if it has to be time to go. Better to go with someone who loves you holding your hand than go all alone or with strangers. She hoped it was true that at the time of passing over, people you had loved who had gone before came to help you make the change. Maybe her own little mother would be there, and the fight about nothing-at-all wouldn't matter any more. Maybe her mother would smile and reach out to take Mary's hand, and maybe Mary would grab on, hard, and squeeze. And in time, when the confusion was finished and Mary was settled in that place, maybe they could sit down and talk about what hadn't been talked about before, and Mary could call her daughter Smoocherooni and be told Smoocherooni-your-own-self. Rowan knew she was crying for herself, not for Mary. Mary Milligan didn't need anything any more, but Rowan Hanson still did, maybe more than ever.

She didn't know about Mary's insurance policies until after the trip out on a gillnetter to scatter the ashes and deep-six the urn. It was in the going through and sorting out of her grandmother's few personal things that Rowan found the will and the policies in a folder with copies of every income tax return the old woman had ever filed. Paper-clipped to the insurance policies was a note scrawled on a ragged-edged piece of writing paper: "Rowan— told you I was worth more dead than alive. I love you. Gran." It hurt even more than the scattering of the ashes. Even in the downturn times, even when jobs were scarce as rocking-horse shit and pogey barely enough to keep the rent paid, Mary had found a way to keep up the premiums. She could have cashed them in at any time, but she kept them paid up even though she had said more times than enough that insurance was nothing but a gamble, and like any gamble, stacked against the fools who thought they could play against the house and win. It hurt but it helped heal, too. Mary had known she'd never benefit from any of this careful scrimping and saving, it was something she had done for Rowan, not because she felt she had to but because she had wanted to do it, wanted it so badly she managed to hang onto it all even after she was sick.

In the city, the two-storey three-bedroom house would have cost one hundred and thirty thousand dollars. In town, it would have been a steal for eighty-five thousand. A hundred miles up-coast, at the end of a dog's breakfast of a highway, after a ferry crossing of a deep fjord, the house and six acres of land, half of it covered with second-growth fir and cedar, cost less than forty thousand. Of course, there was no paved road, no sidewalks, no streetlights and no sewer pipe taking body waste to the ocean. Just a rough dirt road leading from the highway, a culvert and bridge over a wide ditch and two ruts pretending to be a driveway up to the house.

The kitchen sink, the bathroom basin and the bathtub all emptied into the garden halfway down the hill. There was no flush toilet, but a shady path led to a two-holer. Hydro poles brought electricity from the road to the house and the same poles supported the telephone and cable TV lines.

Rowan moved in the same day "spring forward, fall back" took effect and the first thing she did was move her clock an hour ahead. Then she finished unloading the rented truck, carrying boxes into the house and piling them in the middle of what would be her living room.

When the truck was empty she drove back to town with it, returned it to the rental agency, spent one last night in the little rented house, then rolled her sleeping bag, shoved it in the waterproof stuff-sack, put it in the trunk, and headed to her new home and new life, with Babe and Lucky Lou in the back seat. Now that Mary was gone, she wanted as far from sidewalks, fluorescent lights, shopping malls and electrocution cages as she could get.

She got back in plenty of time to start a fire in the Jotul stove, set up her bed and cook a proper supper. She ate, stacked the dishes in the sink, then started opening boxes, putting away dishes, cups, mugs and bowls, deciding where the cutlery was to go, putting Mary's stainless steel cooking pots and pans in their place. She even found the box of sheets and blankets and got her bed properly made before giving in to the total exhaustion. She went outside with the dogs for half an hour, letting them sniff and snuff, squat and pee repeatedly, then she called them in, locked the doors and went to bed, too tired to yawn.

For three days she nested, finding places for her things, struggling to get the chests of drawers up the steep stairs, grunting and cursing the carpet she would never have bought but couldn't discard simply because it had been Mary's prize possession. The fourth day she drove down the highway to the hamlet and found the MiniMart. When she took her groceries home she realized she did feel she was "home." That surprised her. She had expected months of dislocation. Moving had always meant feeling like a visitor, uneasy in the corner store, uncertain in the shoe store, feeling obvious and out of place walking down a new street, certain deep within herself that inside the houses the settled people were looking past their curtains and telling each other the Nomad was walking past their yard, the Stranger was probably lost, again.

Babe and Lucky Lou settled in as quickly as Rowan herself. At first they set off a stink at every little sound, but by the end of the second week they knew their place, knew their duties, and let the squirrels chatter and the ravens scream unchallenged.

There was no Welcome Wagon, and no neighbours came over to introduce themselves or invite her to coffee with 'the girls'. They left her alone and she took the hint and left them alone. But she mucked out the henhouse and found the Farmer's Institute, bought new wire to replace the fence around the hen yard and put a hand-lettered advertisement up on the bulletin board. Someone phoned, and Rowan took directions, then drove six miles to buy half a dozen hens and a rooster. The hens were no sooner settled in their coop than two of them went broody, and by mid-May the chicks were scurrying after their mothers, peeping shrilly.

She gave herself two months to settle in, two months during which she paid no attention to those things in life she had always considered important, two months to spade and plant her vegetable and flower gardens, two months to prepare holes, buy roses and plant them, two months to pee on all her posts and nest herself into a feeling of settled familiarity. Only then did she sit down with a pot of coffee and look at her options.

She had a place of her own and a vehicle which would get her where she wanted to go and back home again for another eight or ten years, barring disaster. She had twenty-five thousand dollars in the bank and few marketable job skills. She had driven taxi and quit because too many drunks considered a woman cabbie an easy mark and too many druggies saw her as a place to get money. One knife too many had flickered in the overhead light. One boyfriend too many had started a slap-show in the back seat of the cab and one girlfriend too many had sobbed for help. Rowan decided she'd make better money answering an advertisement in *Soldier of Fortune* magazine, and quit driving cab, with a promise to herself she wouldn't start driving again unless she was well into her fourth day without a thing to eat.

She knew how to set live traps, she knew how to kill unwanted pets, she knew how to get cats out of trees and down phone poles. She could even coax a budgie bird off a cablevision wire and get it back into a cage. But you don't get a lot of calls to do that, and when you do, nobody pays you much for your skill.

Rowan went to Canada Employment and registered for a job. She checked the board. She bought groceries and chicken feed and went home. In the next two weeks she put in applications at every place she could think of. She waited. While she waited, she put pink fibreglass insulation batting between the floor joists and up in the eaves of the attic. She fixed her porch. She cleaned the eavestroughs and replaced a section of downpiping. There was lots to do. None of it paid wages.

In September she signed on at the college. Two weeks into the course she knew that no matter how well she understood computers, no matter how skillfully she could make them do what she wanted them to do, no matter where she got the job or how well they paid her, it wasn't for her. She hated the hum, she detested the glare from the screen, and something about the damned things made her feel as if her brains were leaking out her ears. But she finished the course. After all, she'd paid enough for it.

Just before Christmas, a cold snap hit. Rowan went into the hardware store and bought heater cables, wrapped her pipes with them and crossed her fingers. You never knew with things like that. They might work, or you might wind up lying on your back under the house with spider webs in your hair, blow-drying your frozen pipes.

The third day one of the neighbours showed up and introduced herself. "Just checking to make sure you're okay."

"Thank you," Rowan smiled, "I think I'll make it. The coffee can be ready in half a shake of a lamb's tail, would you like some?"

"Thank you," the woman smiled. She stepped into the hallway, took off her gumboots and padded across the shiny floors in thick grey wool work socks. "Looks nice in here," she commented. "How'd you get the shine on the floor?"

"Varathane." Rowan filled the coffee maker, added fine ground and went for mugs while the machine burbled and chortled. "I don't know that I'd do it again, though," she confessed. "Not inside the house like that. I did it in the summertime thinking well, at least I can leave the doors and windows open and get rid of the smell. It didn't get rid of the smell and the dust drifted in something fierce. I suppose if I'd done it in the winter I'd have suffocated before it was finished."

"My dear," the neighbour laughed softly, "that's why God made men. To do jobs like that."

"I've thought of that," Rowan said easily, "but they eat so much and when they aren't working they're noisy."

"You don't have to *keep* one," the woman mock-lectured, "you can get them out of the want-ads for practically nothing. Or you can borrow mine for things like that. Six dollars an hour and lunch."

"If the floor needs done again, I might take you up on that. I almost went for tiles or linoleum, but I kind of like those old boards; they aren't hardwood but they sure are pretty."

"You got your pipes done? It's going to freeze, you know. Any time there's as many elderberries on the bushes as there were this year, you can be sure it's going to go down below freezing and stay there a week or two."

"I got heater cables." Rowan put out the chocolate cake and some small plates. "I don't know if they'll work, mind you, but I'm hoping."

"Was it cold where you lived before?" the neighbour asked casually.

Rowan hid a grin. "Same as here," she replied. "I was living just down-coast." She elaborated, telling about her rented house, about Mary's death, about the insurance settlement. "And I just got, I don't know, I got to feeling I had to get something stable and settle down, and I knew unless I won the lottery I couldn't afford to do that where I was."

"You're not from the city," the woman smiled. "We wondered if you were from the city."

"No. Nor any of my family. And," Rowan teased, "we're not Yanks, either."

They laughed then, and Regina stayed almost an hour, eating two pieces of chocolate cake and filling Rowan in on the other neighbours on the road.

The following day, the woman from up the hill came down to introduce herself and stayed half an hour. Rowan showed her the aquarium heater she had put in the chickens' drinking water.

"Won't they peck at it until they break it?" Megan worried.

"I wrapped it in hardware cloth. It's like wire."

"Be nice if it works. Let me know. I get fed up trotting back and forth with warm water. But if you don't, they start to eat snow and then the next thing you know they're sick. It's as bad as having children," she sighed.

When the roads were thoroughly iced, snow began to fall, piling up on the frozen ruts, making travel both interesting and challenging. Rowan piled several bags of sand in the trunk of her car, then, chains flapping and clattering, went into town for groceries. On her way in she stopped to see if Regina needed anything.

It was Regina told Rowan about the job at one of the shucking plants. She just dropped the information into the conversation when Rowan brought back the groceries. Two days later Rowan was standing at a huge cement sink, her feet numb almost to the knees in spite of two pair of socks in her gumboots. For hours she stood on a cold wet cement floor opening oyster shells and scooping out the grey flesh inside. Every so often she put down her shucking tool and went over to where the buckets of warm water waited, and she plunged in her aching hands to warm them. The needling jabs of pain didn't go away but at least she could feel her fingers again. At night her wrists ached, especially the tendon running up her arm from her thumb. But it was a job, and the more you shucked, the more you got paid. She took a hint from some of the other shuckers and bought a rectangle of high-impact foam rubber for the floor beneath her feet. It helped some, but the cold still went up into her calves and knotted the muscles into charley horses and sometimes her foot cramped, particularly in the arch, and she had to sit down and massage the knot out of her muscles.

She worked at the shucking plant four months, and then the angel of mercy took pity on her. Rowan got a job on the ferry between the mainland and the island. Her first day at work, she was told she got the job over all the other applicants because she had her First Aid and had held down a municipal job for three years. "Can't transfer it for seniority, but the ferries are government run and provincial or municipal, government is government. First Aid ticket clinched it."

Before long, her hands stopped aching, the chronic swelling went down, she could move her thumbs without feeling as if pins were jabbing her, and she was putting money back in her depleted savings account.

It was like being somewhere between a grill cook and a server in a delicatessen. Passengers came up the steps from the car deck and turned into the cafeteria, stood in line to get a tray, then moved in orderly fashion past the glass cases of desserts, sandwiches and fruit to where Rowan and one or two others stood smiling and waiting for orders. Clam chowder, soup of the day, burger, today's special, do you have french fries? No? Just potato chips? I'll pass, thanks. They moved on, past the coffee and tea, past the ice cream to the cashier, then paid and took their grub to one of the fixed tables in the large room.

Rowan got teased by her neighbours about getting paid big money to slice pies, but she wasn't a pie slicer, nor did she have a union job scooping mashed potatoes. She and the others were the life-saving crew and without them the federal Ministry of Transport would have beached the entire ferry fleet. They did more than stand behind the steam tables taking orders for chili dogs and hot turkey sandwiches. They practised getting the lifeboats down into the water and took turns figuring out new ways to behave like hysterics so their crewmates could practise coping techniques. Rowan won the Drip of the Month award when she pretended to be the fat woman with the English accent who had lived briefly three houses up in the float camp. She came racing from the cafeteria screeching bloody murder, her arms loaded with lifejackets, then ran in circles hollering Britannia Rules the Waves. Each time someone tried to get hold of her to put her in a lifeboat, Rowan flailed the lifejackets by the canvas tie-straps, aiming for the face, screaming insults and vowing to report the whole bloody flaming lot to the ferry authority. The rest of the crew collapsed in laughter, even the steward. The ship and the entire crew, according to the stop-watch, had gone to the bottom before the hilarity stopped.

"How come if this ferry is publicly owned and I'm part of the public, I have to pay to ride on it?" a wit asked, scowling.

"You have to pay for gas to drive your car down the highway," Rowan smiled, "and then you have to pay for the highway, too. This way you only pay for the gas, and the chauffeur to get you there."

"Oughta build a bridge," he muttered.

"Yes, sir," Rowan agreed. "They've been talking about that bridge for fifty years and one day, who knows, they just might get to it. Then I'm sure they'll put a tollbooth on both ends and we'll all wind up paying to use it, too."

"Right," the grump agreed. "They've always got their hands in our pockets."

"Yes, sir!" Rowan waited, still smiling.

"Is that chowder any good?" he demanded.

"Good? Well, it's hot, I'll say that for it."

"Right," he laughed. "Okay, I'll take some of that hot stuff. Boy, I remember when the clam chowder on these ferries was so good people'd buy a ticket just for the chance to sit down and have a coupla bowls."

"You remember that?" she teased. "Then you must be even older than I am."

"Dolly," he winked, "the entire world is older than you are." He took his bowl and moved on toward the coffee urns and styrofoam cups. Rowan directed the full force of her smile on the next person in line.

The wages were good, the benefits were good and the shifts were easy to get used to. After a while you got to know the regular users and developed a near friendship with them. It was amazing how many people went in one direction or the other every few days. The mail truck driver went over on the last ferry every night and came back on the first ferry in the morning, having slept four or five hours in the back of the van with the parcels and bags of envelopes. The feed store truck driver always wanted Soup of the Day on his weekly crossing. The little guy who drove the stinking clam van took his own lunch with him and only needed a few cups of coffee. He went over every morning on the first ferry, picked up the clams that the Viets and Indians had dug during the night and came back on the three-fifteen run, his van leaking salt water and clam juice.

It was the goddamn tourists made the job a pain in the face. Think nothing at all of standing there blocking the line while they had an in-depth conversation comparing the menu on this ferry to the menu on some other ferry. People behind them shifted uneasily, kids wailed, old people gripped the guard rail patiently, and the tourists just kept talking. At first Rowan tried to be friendly, but after a while she, like all the others, learned how little the tourists respected friendliness, and just called out firmly, "Keep the line moving, don't hold up the line."

Nothing satisfied the tourists. Even the scenery wasn't what they had expected it would be. They hogged the roads with their huge motor homes and expensive camper vans, creeping along as if everyone else in the line-up behind them had nothing else to do with their lives than poke along the highway when it was impossible to pass. The first hint of a straight stretch and they pushed the pedal to the floor and roared along too fast for anyone to overtake them. They never used the turnouts and paid no attention at all to the signs imploring them not to impede traffic. The weather was never to their satisfaction, and the climate seemed to be the sole responsibility of the ferry workers.

"Don't you people ever have sunshine? It's been foggy the whole time we've been here!"

"Is rain all it does around this place?"

"Does the wind always blow this way?"

"No ma'am," Rowan smiled, "sometimes it blows the other way."

When her shift ended, Rowan left the ferry and walked behind the foot passengers to the parking lot. She got in her car, waved to the world and went home.

She changed clothes, whistled for the dogs and headed into the bush for a good long quiet walk with nothing to worry about except maybe bears, cougars and wolves. No tourists.

V

Rowan spoke to him before she knew him as a person. She teased him out of a grisly mood and got him laughing as part of her job, thinking nothing at all about what she did, or who he was. He complained about an increase in ferry fares, spoke scornfully of politicians, then cheered up and asked about clam chowder, and how was she to know anything more would come of it than that?

He took the ferry Tuesday morning, came back Wednesday evening, went over again Thursday morning and came back Friday on the last sailing. Without ever knowing how it happened, Rowan wound up involved with him. There were some who thought she'd hustled him, others who were convinced he'd hustled her, and who knows, maybe everyone was right. Whoever did however to whomever, hustle, tap on or invite, he was just there one day, parked in her driveway, calling to her out the open window.

"Hey, Dolly," he grinned, "is feeding chickens or shovelling hen-house floors the only entertainment you get?"

"What more could a woman want?" she answered, leaning on her shovel and grinning.

He got out of his car, closed the door, then rested against the fender, looking her place over, nodding approval. "Got good water?" he asked, fishing his cigarettes from his shirt pocket.

"Drilled well," she bragged. "Ninety-foot bore hole, and all the water we want."

"Lucky." He offered her a cigarette and she moved forward to take it, leaning the shovel against the slat wall of the compost bin.

"Not luck. I had it dowsed and knew ahead of time there was lots of water."

"You believe that stuff? Dowsing and witching and that?"

"Got lots of water, didn't I? And right where the dowser said it would be."

"Only time I ever had anything to do with one of them he took a wire coat hanger, straightened it out and followed the water pipes from the house to the main connection. I always figured he already knew where they were and was just, like, puttin' on a show for the folks at home."

"All I know is, I've got all the water I'll ever need and it came in where he said it would."

"So you believe."

"Why not? No harder to believe than it is to disbelieve. Easier, actually, if you're standing there watching it happen."

"So what else do you do besides babysit your chickens?" he asked, scratching Babe behind the ears in a casual manner that told Rowan he was used to dogs, knew their likes and dislikes.

"Not much."

"Y'ever go in for a pizza?"

"Not often," she admitted.

"Why'nt you go change your jeans and I'll take you in and buy you the best pizza this side of Edmonchuk."

She hesitated, but only briefly. Then she was nodding, leading the way to the back door, leaving the henhouse for later, and while she showered he sat in the small living room sipping a can of cold pop, leafing through the newspaper she hadn't had time to open and read yet.

Rowan didn't expect anything much to come of it. She'd gone for pizza before, she'd gone for fish'n'chips, she'd even gone for drinks with this one or the other, and she always managed to keep her emotions under control and her soul to herself. Any time in her life she'd heard someone say, "oh, but he's different," she'd laughed, and not always privately. But something did come of it and whatever it was, it was different, and she knew it.

"Jesus, Rowan," Regina said carefully, "are you sure you know what you're doing?"

"No," Rowan admitted, "I haven't got a clue what I'm doing. You trying to tell me the news is bad?"

"Let's just say if it isn't bad it isn't exactly good."

"How so?"

"Complicated is a word I'd use if I had to find one to describe his situation."

Complicated was a good word. There was a divorce in the works, with an angry ex and three surly kids, the youngest ten, the oldest almost fourteen. "I'm not interested in getting involved in any of that," she told him bluntly. "I figure if I'm having a relationship of any kind at all, I'm having it with you; not the ex, the kids, the house, the car, the boat or the lawyer who's apt to wind up with it all, anyway."

"I know that." He nuzzled her neck, stroked his hand up her bare back. "It's just me'n'you, Babe."

"Babe is my dog," she said firmly. "My name is Rowan."

"Ah, c'mon, now, don't be that way."

"I'm that way. Always been that way." But his hand was firm, his skin warm, and his lips were tracing fire down her spine. The skin on his face was smooth, with that tight cleanness of just-after-shaving. It was hard to remember what it was she wanted to say to him, hard to believe what she needed to say was the least bit important, and maybe it wasn't important at all, maybe it was just something bloody-minded and untrusting inside her, something she'd be better off to ignore.

The ten-year-old, Jim told Rowan, had difficulties interrelating with authority figures. "Does that mean she doesn't do what she's told?" Rowan asked mockingly.

"Well, the shrink who saw her said she had decided I was the only person who had any authority over her, and when her mom'n'me split up, she decided even I didn't have any."

"The shrink told you that, eh?"

The eleven-and-a-half-year-old recognized authority figures and never confronted any of them. She just smiled, shrugged, agreed totally and continued to do what she had decided in the first place. "Passive aggression," Jim told Rowan.

"Seems to me just another case of someone who won't do what she's asked or told," Rowan yawned.

"Never had kids, eh?"

"Never wanted any. But I remember being one."

"Yeah." He put his face on her bare belly, his whiskers bristly, his breath warm on her skin. "It wasn't all that long ago, either."

"Dirty old man," Rowan said, sliding from her sitting position against the head of the bed, turning her body to Jim, losing her interest in his passively aggressive kid.

The almost-fourteen-year-old wafted through life with a wide smile on his face, bringing in B-plus marks without ever seeming to do homework, and still managing to be on the soccer, lacrosse, softball and track teams. "He's like I was," Jim grinned. "Whatever's going on, get into it and wind up at the top of the heap."

"Ah, the macho all-Canadian male. Hockey-beer-fuck, in that order. All executive decisions made by wrist-twisting competitions. Ugh, Tarzan big wimp, me king of jungle."

"Wanna live in my tree house?"

"Hell, you don't even have a tree, let alone a house in one."

It was true, Jim didn't have a tree. He didn't have a pot to pee in or a window to toss it out of, and he had all he could do to make the payments on his new car. "I don't know," he shrugged helplessly, his dark eyes looking across the table at her, his fork poking aimlessly at his pancakes. "It was just. . . I don't know. Like one minute I had it all, eh? Family, pile of stuff, money in the bank, job I could depend on. . . and the next minute. . . ker-thunderin'-pow, it was gone!"

"Maybe what you have to do is decide it would have been worth it at twice the price and just go on from here."

"You think so?" He thought about that, forking up pancake with maple syrup, eating hungrily, swallowing before speaking again. "I think you're probably right. It's just, you think you know a person, right? And you have this idea of what your life is and suddenly zip-pop and it's all gone and you don't know what's happened."

"What did happen?" She sighed, not wanting to hear any of this. But he seemed obsessed, and maybe if he had a chance to just spit it out, it wouldn't stick in his throat so much.

"I don't know. I'm sure she's got her story, and I'd bloody well like to hear it so I'd have some idea! All I know is, all of a sudden she's bouncing off the walls like some kind of head case, and nothing I do or say is right. Nothing I think, either, probably. And I come home one night and all my stuff's piled on the porch, and the door is locked. When I try to unlock it to find out what the Christ is coming down, my key don't fit! So rather than give the neighbours a night's free entertainment, I load my crap in my car and go to a motel. And guess what? You do that and it's bloody desertion in the eyes of the lawyers and the court! So here I am. And there she is. And I got less than I had fifteen years ago and she's got the house, the car, the whole nine yards, and the kids."

"There had to be some reason she was coming off the walls."

"Yeah? All I know is what happened. It was like watching someone in one of those horror movies, you know, the hair gets shaggy, the fangs grow, the fingernails go black and turn into claws...except it was slower...and it all happened inside, not outside...I mean it was...like...well, see, when I met her she was in grade eleven and I was friends with her next-door neighbour and we'd all go swimming together and by the time Christmas came, well, there we were and it was all cupids and nosegays and we wanted the white picket fence. So...a person gets older, I guess, and that person wants changes, and I guess what I wanted wasn't the same as what she wanted and...I don't know, Babe, I really don't know. But we went from talking about everything to talking about nothing, just snarling and being teed off with each other," and he looked so puzzled, so hurt, so unable to comprehend that Rowan just let it all slide past because she hadn't really wanted to know anyway.

Rowan didn't go to court the day of the divorce hearing. For one thing, she was on shift, and anyway she figured it didn't have anything to do with her. She got home expecting to go for a walk with Babe and Lucky Lou, then have supper alone before Jim arrived. Instead she found him sitting on her sofa with a glass of rye in his hand.

"I jimmied the window," he said for openers.

"You jimmied the window?" Her sense of invasion and outrage was almost paralyzing, as strong as when you're grabbed from behind by someone you don't know and indecent suggestions are grunted into your ear.

"Yeah. I don't have a key," he reminded her. "And I didn't want to spend another minute in that rat hole room of mine. So..."

"So you came out here with a big bottle of booze and broke into my house so you could sit on my sofa getting drunk and spilling your drink onto my rug." The feeling of paralysis was evaporating, and Rowan was learning for herself what goes on in the thousands of self-defence courses being taught across the country to women who are sick and tired of feeling helpless.

"Ah, hey, it wasn't like that at all. What are you so mad about? What did I do that was so wrong?"

"What am I so mad about? This is *my* house, Jim. This is *my* home. That's *my* window you jimmied! I mean, Jesus, man, you're bleeding all over my life here! You know I don't like drunks, you know I can't handle boozers, you know how I feel about it and you still show up here to tie one on."

"Listen, lady, I got pulled through the wringer today, okay!"

"Yeah, but it was your wringer, not mine." The anger was gone, cold rage had taken its place. Rowan had her own problems, why did she have to have someone else's dropped in her lap for her to solve? There's enough mess in one life for one person to clean up, nobody needs the mess of two or three or five lives.

"Well, that's supportive, isn't it! Thanks a whole helluva lot, Babe."

"Supportive? What the fuck is that supposed to mean? Supportive! I've got all I can handle just keeping myself upright, okay. I can't carry you. I'm not one of those hernia trusses you send off for in the *National Inquirer*. If your balls are sagging, find a way to haul 'em back up but don't expect me to walk around with them cupped in my hand, holding them safe, like they were the crown jewels! I don't like people jimmying my windows."

"I never asked you to *carry* me! I take care of myself!"

"Yeah, you just go around pulling B&E's so you can brood on other people's furniture and maybe have someone there to listen when you start to sing the blues. Maybe we need to have a clear understanding of what the borders of this thing you call a relationship are supposed to be, because as far as I'm concerned it doesn't seem to be what you think it is. Why don't we agree that you can shit your friends and I'll shit my friends and we won't shit each other, okay?"

"Oh, here it comes, more of that west coast banter talk!" He drained his glass and put it down on the little coffee table so hard it didn't clink so much as bang. "You shit your friends," he mocked, "and I'll shit my friends, but we won't shit each other. For someone who doesn't go to bars you sure talk like you grew up in one."

"Which might be exactly why I won't go in them any more," she snapped. "I've heard all the jokes, Jim. I've heard all the sad stories. I've heard boozers singing their somebody done me wrong songs, and it's boring. Bee-oh-ahrr..."

"I can fuckin' spell!" he shouted. "I don't need you to tell me how to spell the word boring. You wanna know what's boring? Listening to your fuckin' sermons is what's boring! It isn't enough I get hauled through the wringer, it isn't enough I get taken to the fuckin' cleaners, it isn't enough I get it hauled out of me in great bloody bleeding hunks, no, I gotta come home to *this*."

"You didn't come *home*," she said coldly. "You broke into *mine!*"

"Have it your own fuckin' way." He got to his feet, weaving noticeably, and headed for the door, knocking over the little table on his way. He scooped a chair out of his way, sent it on its side, opened the door and went out, slamming the door behind him.

Rowan stood shaking with fury, wishing she had some idea of what had happened, wishing she could put into calm, rational words the things she was feeling. Half of her wanted to go after him, yell her version of things until he listened, the other half of her wanted to go after him and apologize. What she did was pick up the rye bottle with the two or so inches of amber fluid on the bottom, unscrew the cap, pour the stinking liquid down the sink, wash it away with cold water, re-cap the bottle and drop it, empty, into the garbage.

"I *hate* hooch!" she shouted to the empty house.

He came back just before midnight, drunk. He pounded on the door and shouted until she got out of bed and went downstairs, turned on the lights and unlocked the door.

"You're drunk," she accused.

"Fuckin' rights," he agreed, pushing past her and wobbling his way to the sofa. "And I might get drunker, too."

"Not here you won't." She moved quickly, snatched the bottle from his hand and fired it out the back door.

"Up yours, too," he laughed, flopping to the couch. "Don't bother me. I won't let it bother me because I'm not gonna fight with you."

"Oh, Jesus," she sighed, "I know exactly what kind of night it's going to be."

"Know what he said? That fuckin' judge? Know what he said? Said I get to see my kids one weekend a month is what he said! And know what else he said? She gets the house. 'The family dwelling' he called it. She gets it. For as long as there's a kid still in school! And if she don't wanna go back to work she don't have to go back to work. I mean, my God! Even if she does go back to work, if she went to work tomorrow, I'd still have to pay her two hundred dollars a month for the first year and a half! Says she needs to 're-establish herself in the work force'. Re-establish my ass, she was never established, she wouldn't know work if it came up and slapped her in the fuckin' eye! A thousand goddamn dollars a month it's gonna cost me what with child support, spousal support and one thing and a bloody other. A thousand a month!" He sighed deeply, glared at the braided rug, wiped his mouth several times, then fumbled for his cigarettes. "Jesus fuckin' wept," he decided.

She knew if she gave him coffee he wouldn't sober up, she'd just have a wide-awake drunk on her hands. She knew if she fried bacon and eggs he'd interpret that as an invitation to stay. And she knew with or without an invitation she wasn't getting him off the sofa before dawn. "I'm not fightin' with you," he said, and she didn't know if it was a warning or a promise. "All's I'm gonna do is kick off my shoes, swing my legs up, cram a pillow under my head and go to sleep. And we'll talk about this some other time."

"And you can't understand why you wound up with a kid who is passive aggressive," she said bitterly. "Another case of apples don't fall far from the horse's ass."

Rowan went to bed angry, but before she fell asleep she felt sorry for him. He looked so baffled, like a bull who has inadvertently shoved his nose into a nest of yellowjackets and cannot understand what is hurting him. He was used to smiling, talking and swinging the other person over to his side, and it hadn't worked in court, but he couldn't understand why. She knew it would do no good at all to point out to him that a thousand dollars a month is five times the square root of sweet bugger nothing when it comes to feeding three growing kids and putting shoes on their feet. Besides, she had no right to say even that much, it was none of her business. What she had the right to say, and what she intended to say a lot about, was the jimmying of the window and the coming back and pounding on the door until she was awake, and went down to open it and let him in before he broke something.

In the morning he was asleep and Rowan prepared for work quietly, not wanting to waken him, not ready for the rehash or the onset of round two. When she came home from work, bleary-eyed and fuzzy-headed from lack of sleep, he was busy in the kitchen, smiling and apparently relaxed.

"I was out of line," he said, his dark eyes meeting hers, the smile widening on his tanned face. "And I don't often do that, I promise." He gestured at the pots on the stove, shrugged engagingly. "This will happen a lot more often than that other, but don't get too used to it." He moved to put his arm around her and kiss her cheek.

"I'd like to talk about last night," she managed.

"If you need to, Babe, I will, but before we get into it I think you should know there won't be a helluva lot I can say except I'm sorry. It was pretty much outta character, but I don't deny I did it, and I'm not tryin' to jump away from responsibility. I just don't truthfully know what I can say about any of it, there wasn't much of a why or why not to it. I was drunk. I'm sorry."

They didn't talk about it, they just had supper together. She complimented him on his meat loaf, he said his mother had taught him when he was thirteen. After the dishes were done he kissed her several times, then went back to his room in town and Rowan had a quick bath, went to bed, and fell into a heavy sleep. She had decided that everyone had the right to make a fool of himself once in a blue moon. After all, it wasn't as if he made a habit of getting into houses other people owned and thought they had locked securely, it wasn't as if he was a regular drunk or came every night or two to kick at the door until the wood showed little dents from the toes of his boots. He'd had a load of crap to get rid of and thought he'd found a safe place to off-heave it, and now he knew she wouldn't stand for it, so it probably would never happen again.

The divorce changed their relationship, but Rowan couldn't have described the change or said how it happened. He was still out of town half the time, she still saw him only a few nights a week, neither of them were talking engagement or marriage or even relationship, but something had changed.

"What I'd like to do," he said, sitting on the top step, looking out over the clearing, sipping his honeyed tea, "come spring, is put some grapevines along the side of the house. There's enough cedar poles on the ground just inside the rim of the bush that I could build a good support arbor for them . . . they'd get good sun all day, and it could be a nice shady spot to sit in when the August bleach-'em-out starts again."

"Grapes would be nice," she agreed. The stair was cold under her butt, a dampness twisting around her ankles. "I'm going in," she told him, "I'm sure summer has taken a bite of the biscuit, it's not comfortable out here after supper any more."

"Yeah, leaves are turning and dropping real fast." He followed her into the house, rubbing his butt and laughing softly. "What kind of a garden do you get here?"

"Not good," she confessed. "It's mostly gravel and rock under that half-inch layer of poor dirt. I refuse," she laughed, "to call it soil. It isn't soil, it's just ground-small rock."

"Build some boxes, get some topsoil from the swamp, mix it good with composted manure and do raised bed intensive," he told her.

She stared at him, then shook her head, puzzled. "You know how much a board costs?" she asked. "I bought a seven-foot plain ordinary old pine board because I wanted to fix a shelf in the pantry. That board cost me eleven dollars. One board! And it wasn't some fancy kind of pine, it was about the cheapest board in the place. Eleven dollars and even then it had a twist in it. You got any idea how much those boxes you're talking about would cost? Then the rest of it, hoses and sprinklers and . . . I can buy fresh organic stuff at the Farmers' Market for years on what it's going to cost just to get a garden started! And someone else is doing all the work, too."

"Ah, come on, what've you got your own place for if you can't even have a garden?"

"I have a full-time job. If I've got any energy left in what we laughingly call spare time, I want to use it for things I enjoy. Like fishing."

"Helluva way to kill worms." He finished his tea, shaking his head, teasing her. "Didn't anyone tell you a boat is just a hole in the water into which you pour money?"

"I don't have that kind of boat," she laughed, thinking of her rowboat, "and I don't have that expensive kind of fishing gear, either. But I've got lots of fish in my freezer."

"Well, just the way you buy veggies, I buy fish. And just the way you like to go fishing, I like to grow veggies. See, between the two of us we're gonna save a fortune on food, Babe."

"Babe is the dog," she reminded him for what seemed like the ten thousandth time.

By Christmas he was staying at her place so many nights it seemed stupid for him to keep paying rent on a room he hardly ever used. Besides, money was tight and it boiled down to either he saved the rent money or he had to find a part-time job, which would mean he would hardly ever see her, and when he did, he would be tired. So he moved his stuff to her place and went to work from there. It didn't make much change in her life, really, nothing you could point to or measure, but it altered almost everything. She became aware of things she hadn't known or wanted to know.

"Hell!" He slammed his car door and walked to the back steps, his shoulders slumped, his face glum. "I get there and nobody's home."

"You're kidding." Rowan threw the ball and the dogs raced after it, shouldering each other, pushing, each trying to get to the red rubber prize first.

"Not a soul. Maybe the cat, but I'm not sure cats have souls. So another weekend visit goes up the tube!"

"I thought it was last weekend you were supposed to visit them."

"Well, I couldn't, could I? Fuckin' *told* her... what a witch!"

She almost asked if he had phoned before visitation day to explain, she almost asked if he had arranged to switch weekends, she almost asked any of a dozen obvious questions, but she didn't want the whole day going into yet another rehash of how bitchin' miserable it all was, so she just let it glide past and tossed the drool-slippery red rubber ball across the driveway for the dogs to chase.

She couldn't for the life of her figure out what his ex was doing, or why she would want to do it, and the only thing Rowan herself knew for sure was that she didn't want any of it ever to be any of her business. Sometimes, when he went over to visit with his kids, they were waiting and he spent the day with them, doing God alone knows what, although it all seemed to require a pocketful of money and one or the other of them must eat sneakers, the number of new pairs that needed to be bought. Sometimes the phone would ring and it would be for him. He'd sit with the receiver to his ear, sighing, nodding and talking softly. Rowan concentrated on the television and made sure she hadn't the foggiest notion what the byplay meant. Sometimes he would leave for his access visit and be back again in no time at all, usually glum, sometimes shaking with fury. She knew he wanted to explain to her,

she knew he wanted to talk to her about it and she knew she didn't
want to hear a word.

"You might try being a bit of help once in a while," he accused.

"I told you," she said easily, "it's not my pain in the ass, it's yours. If
I had ever wanted problems like that, I could easy enough have had my
own. I don't even *know* your ex, why would I want to take sides in a
fight with her?"

"I don't know anybody else has a girlfriend who won't take any
interest at all in the kids."

"Ah, but that's what you said you liked about me," she teased. "I'm
different, remember?"

"Bill Henley's girlfriend has his kids over from Friday night until
Sunday night."

"Good for her. Which means *she* winds up looking after them on the
weekend and his ex looks after them all week and what, pray tell, does
Bill Henley do?"

"Oh, for Chrissakes, I give up!"

"I wish you would," she muttered.

Christmas sped at them like an out-of-control locomotive. The
entire kid-in-the-haypile thing had never meant much to Rowan,
especially after her grandmother's death, and the sudden unexpected
demands almost blew her mind. "Me?" she gaped. "Oh, no, Jim, you've
got entirely the wrong person. I don't ski, I don't want to learn to ski,
if I want a broken leg I can probably arrange one some other, warmer
way! I don't want to spend God knows how much money to rent what
they call a condominium and is probably a glorified and poorly insulated
icebox. I'm not interested in cooking a huge dead bird to feed a bunch
of people I haven't even seen before, and I'm not very interested in
seeing them, whether I cook for them or not. You just arrange yourself
around the things you want to do with them, and I'll just arrange myself
around my own schedule. I'm working the whole time anyway, and
that's the way I like it."

"Working? The whole time? What in hell's wrong with your
union?"

"Nothing's wrong with the union. If it had been important to me I
could have arranged something else, but it isn't important, and there's
other people have kids or grandkids and they want the time off, so I
switched some shifts around and I'm not only going to get statutory

holiday time and a half, I'm going to get time off some time I want it or need it."

"But Jesus, it's Christmastime!"

"Bah, humbug," she laughed. "You know the old joke, huh, about the woman who goes out on her porch to talk to the trespassers and winds up saying 'I don't give a shit what star you think you're following, get those camels off my front lawn!' Well, I agree with her."

"But I wanted to put up a tree in the living room."

"Put it up if you want, just be sure to take 'er down again before the needles all fall off and the bare sticks start to rot."

"I wanted the kids to come over and..."

"Hey, give your head a shake, okay? I don't know how to tell you any nicer, and I don't know how to get through to you, but I am *not* interested in family rah rah rah. You want to have time with your kids, fine, have time with your kids, but don't think bringing them here to meet me is a good idea. I won't fall in love with them, I won't be knocked on my ass by a sudden yearning to mother, and I probably won't impress them one little bit. I told you, I'll be working. So buy the dead bird, stuff it, truss it, roast it and have yourselves a good time. I'll be at work."

"But they want to meet you."

"No they don't," she guessed, "you want them to meet me and they don't know how to get out of it. Cut me some slack on this one, okay? I'll be working. If you want them over here, fine, but it'll be your show, not mine. I don't even mind if they're still here when I get home, as long as the din doesn't keep me from getting to sleep. And," she headed to the bathroom, "I don't intend to get into the swap-goodies routine, either. Tell them I do not want presents and I do not intend to go out and buy any."

"Jesus Christ, Rowan!" he mourned, but she was busy running a nice hot bath and barely heard him over the sound of the water.

The thorn bush dropped into her life by the birthday of the Prince of Peace was effectively removed a week and a half before the big event. Rowan was ironing her uniforms for work, listening to Rosalie Sorels, only peripherally aware Jim was dialling the phone. And then she was startled almost to the point of dropping the steam iron by the roar of his voice as he exploded verbally. "What the fuckin' hell do you mean? Of *course* I expect them to be with me for Christmas! For Chrissakes, it's *Christmas*! I don't give a flyin' fuck *what* you thought you had planned, I'm *tellin'* ya . . ."

When Rowan finished ironing her shirts and touching up her pants, the screaming match was still going full bore. She unplugged the iron, set it on the drainboard to cool, folded the ironing board and put it away in the pantry. By then the iron was cool enough to take to its little place on the shelf. And the fit was still being flung into the phone. She went to the bedroom and closed the door, suddenly tired, knowing Jim had done more talking to the one who didn't want to hear it than he had spent talking to his ex or even to his kids, and he'd done his planning without checking with them any more than he'd checked with her. But she didn't care. She just wanted some peace and quiet.

When he came to bed he was stiff with anger and she knew he wanted to off-load it in her direction.

"You don't have to worry about having your space invaded at Christmas," he said coldly.

"I wasn't worried." She made sure her voice was casual, pleasant.

"They aren't coming," he said, shooting her a sideways dart from his cold eyes. Rowan just nodded. "My plans," he added bitterly, "don't seem to count for shit with anyone!" She bit her tongue and said nothing about making sure any plans were shared with the ones supposedly involved. "Merry fuckin' Christmas!" He flopped to the mattress and turned on his side, his back to her. She sighed, turned out the light and lay on her side with her back turned to him.

She came home from a double shift and the house was quiet. Only the two dogs greeted her. The place was warm, blessedly peaceful, and she made herself a cup of tea, then flopped onto the sofa to watch television. After a while she got up, fed the dogs and let them out to romp in the icy darkness, and it was their scratching at the door to be let in wakened her. "Hey, there," she yawned, closing the door and reaching for the string mop to clean their muddy pawprints from the linoleum. "Remind me to get you some gumboots and teach you how to put 'em on and take 'em off again."

She got up in the morning, showered, got dressed and turned the dogs out into their own yard, with a doghouse liberally floored with hay to protect them from the weather. "Another double shift," she warned them, putting their food and water bowls near the doghouse, "but this is the last one for a while so things'll look up for you soon enough."

When she got home they were still in their yard, the food eaten, the water bowls half filled, a skim of ice forming around the edges.

Jim came home the evening of the day after Boxing Day. Rowan had just finished her supper and was cleaning up the kitchen when the back door opened and he came in looking subdued and apologetic.

"I shoulda phoned, I guess," he said for openers.

"No big deal," Rowan shrugged, then realized with surprise she meant it. She finished rinsing the few dishes, then left them to dry in the plastic coated drainboard. Jim stared at her, blinking with surprise.

"Don't you want an explanation?"

"Not particularly."

"I was visiting friends," he offered.

"That's nice," she smiled. She even kissed his cheek, then snapped her fingers for the dogs. "I'll be back in an hour or so, I'm taking the dogs to the beach for a good run," she told him.

When Rowan got back, Jim was watching a television program that didn't interest her the least little bit, so she went to bed. She was asleep before he came to bed, and he was still asleep when she left for work in the morning. She saw him on the afternoon run, and they had time for a brief chat before she had to get back to the steam table and spoon gravy onto the turkey and cranberry jelly Hot Sandwich Special.

"They want me to take the 'B' run," he told her. "Just for a couple of weeks, then it'll be back to normal. I guess," he grinned, "the festive season was a bit rough on some people."

"I told you," she teased, "you're better off with bah humbug. You get more rest that way."

Driving home, she had the queerest thought. She had four days off coming and as clear as a bell she heard a voice in her head say Oh well, you can sleep in late and then wake up, have a coffee, and cry all damned day if you want to. And that was stupid because what reason did she have to cry?

She had been living with Jim a year and a half when she finally met the oldest kid. Justin was sixteen by then, tall, slender and smiling. He was sitting on the porch when Rowan arrived home from work, and behind him, near the door, was a backpack almost as tall as he was and a suitcase big enough to hold a grand piano and the kitchen of the guy who tuned it.

"Hi," he grinned. He stood up, hands stuffed in his pockets. "You must be Rowan."

"You know more about me than I do about you," she answered, moving to let the dogs out of their yard. "What's your name and how come you're squatting on my porch?"

"I'm Justin, and I'm here to see my dad."

"Your dad won't be home until midnight."

Babe and Lucky Lou came ripping out of their enclosure, leaping to lick Rowan's hands and face, whipping around the house, stopping to sniff and lick Justin's hands before tearing off into the bush to scare the squirrels and enrage the ravens and Stellars jays.

"Great dogs," Justin smiled. "I was going to let them out so they could play but then I figured maybe I'd better not, there must be some reason you put them in that yard when you leave."

"Oh, there's a very good reason I put them in the yard," she agreed. "Babe would just flop on the porch and sleep but Lucky Lou would go for a four-day run or decide to chase cars or something. She's about one-tenth the dog her mother is," she confessed.

"Doesn't say much for her father, does it?" Justin grinned again and stepped aside so Rowan could unlock her back door. She knew he was going to follow her inside but she couldn't think of a way to discourage him, and nobody could leave somebody else just sitting on the porch until midnight.

She made tea and they drank it in a strange kind of silence that was neither relaxed nor tense. Each knew the other knew exactly what their situation was, but neither wanted to speak of it. They just waited for Jim to come home and sort things out for them.

She had pork chops thawed and marinating in the fridge, she peeled potatoes and put them on to boil, she opened a jar of applesauce and steamed frozen green beans. She considered making a salad and rejected the idea. If there wasn't enough food, he'd just have to fill up on bread and gravy.

"This is good," he told her, mopping gravy and finding room in his face for half a slice of bread. She wondered if he chewed or if he just sucked it all in, the way a vacuum cleaner sucks up a pile of under-the-bed dust bunnies.

"There's ice cream in the freezer if you want dessert."

"Great!" He finished his supper, stood up and looked toward the freezer. "You want some?"

"I think I'll pass, thanks."

"You're the boss."

She sat in the big chair watching him ladle ice cream into a cereal bowl, trying to imagine what an X-ray would show; maybe a little tunnel going from the bottom of his stomach to one of his very long legs. Maybe if you could fill the leg with sand he wouldn't pack away so much food.

Justin finished his ice cream and then, without being told, got up and cleared the table, washed the dishes and left them in the drainboard to dry. He even wiped the table and tidied the counters, then stared at the compost bucket.

"What do I do with that?" he asked.

"Chickens," she told him.

"Oh yeah? Wow," he laughed, "so you give them the garbage and then tomorrow morning you get it back as eggs, huh? Man, that's recycling taken to its ultimate."

"Well, you know what they say, what goes around comes around."

"And then goes around again, I suppose. Okay, next question. Do chickens bite?"

She thought he was kidding, but he wasn't. She assured him chickens did not bite and he took the compost bucket outside. He came back a few minutes later with the bucket and put it in the sink. She supposed it could wait a few minutes, then she'd rinse it clean herself.

Justin sat on the sofa, then leaned, then kicked off his sneakers, swung up his legs and half lay, his feet mercifully clear of the doily on the arm of the couch. "Nice place," he said, looking around and nodding approval. "Kind of funky. Like, you'd know it was way out in the country even if you hadn't driven here, right?"

"Way out in the country?" she laughed. "We're only fifteen minutes from downtown!"

"Yeah, but that's some fifteen minutes, I have to tell you. Guess a guy would pretty well need a car, right? To get to school and all, I mean."

"There's a school bus," she corrected, "and there's always your thumb."

"Yeah, but you know how it is with the thumb, it doesn't always work very well. I thought I was going to wind up footing it the whole way here. Hasn't anyone ever thought of flattening out that hill?"

"I was going to do it myself first time I got a century or two with nothing else to do."

"Right," he agreed, "but time don't fly fast enough." He nodded again as if he had experienced everything the world had to offer. Twice.

Rowan went to bed at her usual time, leaving Justin watching TV in the living room. Five minutes after she crawled between the sheets she heard the fridge door open, and knew the leg was hollow again. When Jim finally crawled into bed, she was asleep, and when she left in the morning he was asleep. So was Justin, curled on his side in a sleeping bag on the living room floor, Babe sprawled across his feet, Lucky Lou grinning from where she was curled against his back.

When she snapped her fingers, the dogs got up slowly and obediently to follow her outside. She let them run in the yard while she stood on the steps sipping her coffee, watching the first light play games with the mist and fog weaving between the trees. She finished her coffee, left her empty cup on the top of the propane barbecue, put the dogs in their yard with plenty of water and drove to work, deliberately blocking her thoughts.

When she got home, the dogs were out of their yard. She opened the back door, and they came forward to meet her, tongues lolling, tails thrashing happily. Justin grinned at her from the kitchen, then went back to mixing vegetables for the salad he was creating.

"Hey, Babe," Jim grinned, busy with the mixer, whipping the potatoes to a light froth. "How was your day?"

"One of the tourists suggested it would be a good idea to have a hard bar on the ferry and maybe some slot machines to pass the time."

"Great idea," Justin agreed, "then the fuckers could lose all their money while they were getting drunk enough to kill themselves on that cow track the government calls a highway. And . . ." He held out a slice of green pepper, and Rowan took it and popped it in her mouth. "Look at the money the towing companies would make hauling the wrecks back up out of the toolies."

"Local initiative," she nodded. "Almost as good as secondary industry."

Justin slept with the dogs the second night, too. It felt weird to have to close your bedroom door before you dared snuggle up to your old man, and the sex wasn't as good when you had to remind yourself not to make any noise because someone might be awake downstairs. But millions of people, she told herself, adapt to this, adjust to this, even think it's how things should be.

"So when is he leaving?" she asked.

Jim squirmed, reached for his cigarettes and lit one before trying to answer. "Well," he hedged, "there's a bit of a problem around that."

"Maybe I could be let in on it," she suggested. "This is, after all, my house and that is, when all is said and done, my sleeping bag he's lying in, sweating no doubt."

"He doesn't get along very well with his mother."

"He won't get along at all with me," she warned. "And he isn't staying."

"Ah, come on, Rowan, just for a few days."

"He's been here about as long as I can make myself feel he's welcome."

"What's he done to tick you off?" Jim glared. "He's trying real hard!"

"Let him go home and try that hard with his mother."

"Just give me a day or two to work something out," he begged. "Maybe I can arrange room and board for him with friends in town. He's a good kid!"

"Sure he is. They all are. But I don't want any of them, I never wanted any of them, and I've been about as hospitable as I want to be."

"Yeah." He pulled his arm from under her head and rolled on his side, his back to her. "And it is, after all, your house, right?"

"Something like that," she agreed, rolling on her side, her back to him. She was almost asleep when Jim spoke again.

"I could build a sort of bunkhouse on the edge of the property and they'd be out of your way."

"They? What they? I thought we were talking *him*," she hissed.

"They're my *kids!*" he sat up, angry.

"That's right. They are *your* kids. It isn't where he sleeps is the issue; it's where he *is*."

She heard him sigh deeply, then again, and she felt both angry and guilty. Just when she was starting to feel cheap, low-down and unreasonable, she heard the click of his lighter as he lit yet another cigarette. "I guess if you've never had kids," he said sadly, "you don't know what it's like to have them. And I guess if you don't know, there's no way anyone else can tell you. Just gimme a few days and I'll work it all out somehow. But I can't just toss him out in the snow!"

"There isn't any snow," she grumbled, "it all melted weeks ago."

"Rowan, for Chrissakes, do they give medals for being hard-nosed and are you trying for first place?"

"This thing about your kids comes up time and time again, as if nothing I say is clear, nothing I explain gets heard. This is *your* problem. This is not *my* problem. I see no reason why I should learn to walk around my own place stepping over hollow legs and making room in my house for people I never invited. If he doesn't want to live with his mother, or won't live with his mother, or his mother has shown him the door, or whatever it is that's going on, then *you* have to do more than say 'Rowan do this, Rowan do that'. Don't *talk* about finding room and board for him. Find it! Don't think that having him around for a day, or two, or three, or ten will convert me to motherhood because it won't. What it will do is make me damned angry!"

"Jesus!"

Thursday night, while Jim was out of town with the truck, Justin approached the unspoken issue. "If you had a kid," he started, "and the kid wanted to quit school, what would you say?"

"How old is this kid?"

"Say sixteen."

"And what grade has this kid finished?"

"Finished ten and into eleven."

"I'd tell this kid to take the idea of quitting school and push it where the sun never shines," she answered flatly. "I'd point out to this kid that he-she-or-it has no idea at all what the word 'work' means but with that education and that amount of experience, 'work' would involve a shovel. And just so that kid knew what a shovel was, I'd hand him one and tell him to dig me a ditch from the top of the driveway to the bottom, all along one side, and to have the job done in three days." It was unreasonable, she knew. Nobody could dig that ditch without a backhoe, but Justin didn't have to know that. "And I'd make sure that kid knew that for the rest of his life this is what he'd have to look forward to, eight hours a day, five days a week, and for minimum wage the whole time."

The silence stretched. Justin nodded. He licked his lips a few times, then nodded again, his face sad. "What if the reason this kid wants to quit school is because everyone is broke all the time?" he asked, his voice soft, his long dark eyelashes blinking rapidly against tears.

Rowan sat beside Justin and patted his knee softly. "I'd tell him that being broke in high school is a bitch, but being broke for the rest of your life is worse. And I'd point out there's a lot of part-time work a person can do. Babysitting is a start. Working at the corner store. What I'd do is find out how many old people live in the neighbourhood, then I'd go to each one, knock on the door, introduce myself, tell them I'm a damn fine hand with a lawn mower and pruning snippers. I'd tell them I'd be overjoyed at the chance of work. I'd offer to clean rain gutters, clean basements, clean chimneys, go get their groceries, walk their dogs, scrub the floors, whatever they need done. I'd dig more goddamn gardens than the peasants in China, if that was what it took to make a few dollars. And when I had some steady customers, I'd go to the manager of every apartment building within an hour's walk and tell them I'd be glad to go into an apartment any time anyone moved out and I'd do walls, and floors and windows and . . . you know how hard it is to find someone will do a good job on windows?"

"Yeah?"

"Come on, I'll show you a squeegee."

She and Justin did the windows and the sliding glass door, did them again, then again, just to be sure he knew what to do with the squeegee. Something sharp and jarring between them dissolved in the second bucket of clean water and they could laugh as if they meant it. Rowan knew he was a good kid, she knew they could be friends, she knew it wasn't Justin himself sticking in her throat, it was Assumption, and Expectation, it was the fact that Jim had thought nothing at all of heading off to work as usual knowing Justin would wind up with Rowan. And if that wasn't Justin's fault, it wasn't Rowan's either. And maybe a sixteen-year-old apprentice window washer isn't a baby who needs his diapers changed, and maybe the windows had needed doing anyway, and maybe who knows what or even cares much, the bloody Assumptions were there and she was gagging on them.

"So how does this guy convince his mother that the world won't end if he lines up all these jobs?"

"He waits until she's alone and then he sits down, like an adult, and he tells her what he has in mind," she said firmly. "And when she says no, he doesn't yell or scream or bitch or whine. And she'll say no because, Justin, you are her son. She wants you to have the TV dream life; even though she knows it is impossible, that is what she wants.

She does *not* want to feel her kid has to work! And so you just wait. And a few days later you sit down and you say, Look, here's my schedule at school. My marks won't drop. I've got this study period and that library period and I'll have my homework done or I'll quit the jobs. But I'm better off, you're better off, we're better off if I'm making two-fifty an hour than if I'm farting around kicking a soccer ball."

"Two-fifty an hour? Two-lousy-fifty an hour?"

"Yeah," she nodded, not smiling. "Life doesn't give big money to guys who don't have their ticket."

"Fuck," he sighed.

"Fuck for sure. You'll start looking at things differently. Instead of saying Oh well, what the hell it's only thirty bucks, you'll be saying, Okay, at two bucks an hour that's fifteen hours, and that means I'll have to work two full weekends to pay for it . . ."

"Fuck."

"Nobody ever said it better," she agreed.

Justin stayed three weeks, then moved back in with his mother. If he had any hard feelings about being shown the road by Rowan, he kept them to himself. Alys, however, let Rowan know she deeply resented not being allowed to move her stuff into the house. "Justin stayed," she said stubbornly.

"Not long," Rowan said firmly into the phone. "And you're not even staying that long. You make it up with your mother. Or phone the group home and move in there."

"But *why?*" Alys demanded.

"Because," Rowan said coldly, "none of this is *my* problem, okay? I got along fine with *my* grandmother, you can learn to get along with your mother."

"Yeah, well, if you're so easy to get along with why did you live with your grandma, why didn't you live with *your* mom?"

"She died when I was born," Rowan snapped. The silence lengthened and then Alys sniffled a few times before hanging up the phone. She called back the next day, when Jim was home and Rowan was at work. Rowan came home to an empty house and no sign of supper. She didn't have to be told where he was, or why. She just made macaroni and cheese and enjoyed every bite of it, too. He came home just before midnight, sat on the edge of the bed, looked at her as if he had six thousand things to say, but said none of them. What he did say was

"She's only fourteen." Rowan shrugged and the whole matter dropped into a deep hole.

Jim built his raised beds, planted his seeds and tended his garden. Rowan went to work, looked after her dogs, kept the house clean, did the laundry and, when she had the time, went out in the rowboat to mooch for fish. Summer flared on them, hotter and hotter each day. The ferry traffic was backed up two sailings at every terminal, and overtime was the norm, not the exception.

"This is for my share of the groceries." Jim handed her some money and she smiled and put it in her pocket without counting, at ease with the entire world on the sweaty afternoon of a rare day off. "Wish it was more," he continued, looking down at his toes where they stuck out of his leather sandals. "But the kids needed clothes. . . shoes. . . the whole nine yards."

Rowan nodded, reached out and idly rubbed his tanned, hairy leg. The skin behind his knees was soft, smooth, and there was a place on each of his inner thighs where the stiff denim of his jeans rubbed off the fuzz that covered most of his body.

He sat next to her in the shade of the small Japanese plum tree, grinned down at her and rubbed her bare back. "One of these days," he promised, "I'll win the 6/49, and when I do you'll get every cent I owe you because that bloodsucking witch won't have any claim on it!"

"I'd be using electricity and propane whether you were here or not," she yawned. "Want to go up to the lake for a swim?"

"Sure," he agreed, "we'll take my truck."

It was a new one, black with red upholstery. The radio brought in either FM or AM, and the tape deck was excellent. As soon as she got into the car, Rowan turned down the volume, because Jim always had it turned up so high the seat vibrated. Sometimes the music was just too much, she couldn't tell if they were coming or going, and she didn't know how he could drive in the din without having one accident after another.

The lake was cloudy, the silt kicked up from the bottom by thrashing feet, diving and cannonballing kids who whooped and yelled until even the Stellars jays gave up and flew off, defeated. Rowan swam out to the logs and climbed up on them, balancing awkwardly, then dove back into the water and swam to shore again. Some of the kids were racing along the logs as steady as any boom bozo, and she remembered the time, how many years ago, when she too could move without having to think where she was putting her feet.

She lay on the sun-warmed rock, watching a dragonfly zizzing back and forth, back and forth, its metallic blue body gleaming in the hot afternoon brightness. Jim came out of the water grinning, and reached for the towel.

"Hey, how ya doin'?" A teen-ager separated himself from a group of others who were passing something suspicious from one to the other. Justin's grin was a bit off-centre and his eyes looked as if he'd been swimming underwater in chlorinated water. He flopped to the rock beside Rowan and squinted up at his father. "Thought you musta been outta town or something," he said cheerfully, "either that or died and nobody told us."

"What are you doing with that pack of dope-sucking layabouts?" Jim growled.

"Hey, easy on old boy, them's m'friends," Justin drawled. "So, how's life treating you?" he turned to Rowan.

"Oh, you know how it is," she answered, watching Jim frowning down at his son.

"No, how is it?"

"Well, life's a bitch and then you're dead, I guess."

She sat up, reached for the backpack and pulled out a couple of cold cans of pop. Jim shook his head but Justin took one, grinning, and snapped the tab. He flicked it off the rock and into the water, where it spiralled down to the silt, and was lost.

"You workin'?" he asked easily.

"All the time," she answered. "Tourist season, you know. Half of California and most of Illinois seems to have headed here this year."

"Oh." Justin drank deeply, then looked at his father and held out the can of pop. Jim frowned and shook his head. "I thought somehow you'd been laid off or something."

"Me?" Rowan laughed. "They can't run the ferry without me. I'm the only one owns a wrist watch, without me they'd never be on schedule. What are you doing for the summer? Just hanging out getting fat?"

"I wish!" He crumpled the pop can and placed it on the rock, upside down, to drain. "I work at the fish farm. Great job! You get to feed hormone-enriched pellets to captive salmon, and you also get to haul dead fish out of the pens and take 'em off to a landfill to bury them. But," he sighed, "it pays, and I guess beggars can't be choosers, right?"

"But you're going back to school in the fall, right?"

"Oh yeah. Finish up the old grade twelve, then probably work full time at the fish farm instead of just working summers."

"You really want to do that? I mean, it sounds as if you hate the job."

"I do. But," he shrugged, staring at his father with a tight grin, "like I said, choice hasn't got a lot to do with anything. Poverty, someone told me, is God's punishment for having been so stupid as to have chosen poor parents. Guess I goofed." He stared briefly at Rowan as if about to say or ask something, then he smiled gently. "Thanks for the pop. It's been a slice, eh?"

Rowan watched him head back to his friends, appropriate the new joint and suck deeply at it. Jim flopped beside Rowan, frowning terribly. "Little bastard," he grumbled, "hanging out with that bunch of do-nothing go-nowhere losers. Someone should kick his ass for him."

"Come on," she suggested, "why don't we go home. Out of sight, out of mind, maybe. What you don't see won't put you in a bad mood."

They barbecued a salmon and had it with potato salad, then sat awkwardly on the porch, holding fresh peaches and trying to eat them without dripping juice all over themselves. The phone rang and Jim moved quickly, flipping his peach pit at her and going inside, wiping his hands on his tee shirt.

Whatever the phone call was about, it didn't improve his mood any, and when he finally came back out on the porch he was tight-lipped and squinty-eyed. There was only one person could get to him like that, and although Rowan supposed it would make him feel better to unload some of it on her, she really didn't want to hear about it.

"Jesus," he sighed, "I don't know what that goddamn woman wants. She got everything! I've got holes in my goddamn socks trying to keep her in the style she seems fuckin' determined to get accustomed to, and she's still nagging and bitching at me."

"Hmmm," Rowan said, rising and collecting the plates, forks and peach pits.

"Do you realize if I had to pay rent I'd probably starve?" His voice was loud, his face flushed.

"Well, don't go overboard," she tried to tease him out of it, "you don't pay rent and nobody who's got a belly full of barbecued salmon can claim to be on the brink of starvation."

"Oh, thanks Rowan, thanks a lot. I really appreciate your under-standing and support."

"Yeah?" She felt her smile tighten. "Well, enjoy it while it lasts, darling, because I feel it wearing thin already."

It blew over before bedtime, though. They just ignored it as they had learned to ignore so many other spits and claw sharpenings. They slept curled together with only a sheet over them, and in the morning he left for work without waking her.

She was on her second cup of coffee, sitting on the steps watching the dogs tugging at an old inner tube, dragging each other back and forth across the yard, growling as if they were on the brink of war, their tails wagging happily, when the phone broke the peace. Rowan an-swered casually. "Hay-low, and congratulations, you're my wake-up call."

"Is that Rowan Hanson?" a voice asked.

"You've got it," she replied, "but if you want to sell me something, forget it, I've got a vacuum cleaner, I don't need a freezer or a food plan and I can't read so wouldn't have any use for a set of encyclo-pedias."

"I'm not trying to sell you anything." The woman had about as much sense of humour as a wet toilet seat. "I'm Sue Edwards. I used to be Jim's wife."

"Oh, really." Rowan pulled a face and put her coffee mug on the window sill. "Well, Jim's not here," she said firmly. "He left about three hours ago and he won't be back until tomorrow night."

"I know," Sue said, equally firmly. "I wanted to talk to you."

"Lady," Rowan said, knowing she sounded fatigued and bored, "I'm really not sure any of this is any of my business, but I am sure I don't want to get involved in it."

"You're already involved!" the voice snapped. "My kids are walking around in worn-out shoes because of your involvement."

"Whoa, Nelly!" Rowan yelled. "Don't lay that one on me! Their feet and their shoes are none of my affair."

"They are when their maintenance doesn't come because he has to help pay to get your car fixed."

"Bullshit," Rowan blurted.

"Really? Well, maybe it is and maybe it isn't. Justin said you told him you hadn't been laid off the past few months, is that true?"

"I've never been laid off in my life," Rowan answered, "not that I think it's a whole helluva lot of your business."

"Put on the coffee," Sue said coldly, "because I'm coming over," and she hung up.

Something must have gone wrong with the filters, because the coffee tasted like oily molasses. Rowan sat pretending to drink it, looking at the photocopies Sue had spread on the table.

"I'm not a fool," Sue said gently. "I lived with that guy for almost seventeen years, I know what he's like. And that's why I got the judge to order that the payments be made to Family Court, to be forwarded on to me. And you can see how many payments he's made."

"Jesus, I hope you aren't going to suggest I ought to make them," Rowan sighed, "because I really don't want to have a fight with you."

"Whose new truck is it, yours or his?"

"Well, it's not mine," Rowan laughed. "The old beater is mine."

"And you've been working and supporting yourself?"

"Lady, other than my grandmother, when I was a kid, nobody has supported me."

"Please don't call me 'lady'. We had a dog named Lady once."

"Sorry." And then Rowan looked at the woman across the table from her, really looked. She realized with a slowly growing kind of pity that Sue wasn't much older than Rowan herself. She looked older, though, older than Rowan and older than she really was. She had lines fanning out from the corners of her eyes, and tiny hints of lines around her mouth, as if keeping a stiff upper lip had turned into a total face-ache. Her deep blue eyes looked tired, the kind of tired that can't be repaired by a few hours' sleep, and her hands were not the hands of someone who spent each afternoon buffing her nails.

"Where do you work?" Rowan asked.

"Where I've always worked," Sue said bitterly. "In the oyster plant, shucking the little darlins out of their shells."

"I didn't know," Rowan admitted. "That's mean work; I know, I did it for a while myself. At Sorenson's plant."

"I'm at Mermaid. And you're right, it's mean work. Does he pay rent here?"

"No."

"Does he pay the hydro or the phone or . . ."

"Not that it's any of your business, but no. He helps with the groceries."

"Do you need help meeting the mortgage on this place?"

"I don't have a mortgage, it's all paid off."

"Wish mine was," Sue managed a grin. The grin touched a chord in Rowan she didn't want touched, it established a connection she didn't want established, and she felt herself recoil, then leap as far away as she could get.

"I'm not going to ask what this is all about because I think I know," she blurted. "It's none of my business, and I'm not going to make it my business. And I wish to God we could find something else to talk about. Want another coffee?"

"Thank you, you make damn fine coffee."

"It tastes like shit." Rowan wiped at the tears sliding down her face.

"I've never tasted shit," Sue said, patting Rowan's hand. "Well, that's not true, I've eaten plates full of the stuff, served by the same asshole who ruined your coffee."

"So where's his money going to?" she wailed.

Sue said nothing, just looked off at the wall, and Rowan was forced to think it out for herself. The new car that got traded in on the new truck. Out of town as much as he was at home.

"His weekend visits?" she dared.

Sue shrugged. "Sometimes he makes them, sometimes he doesn't. Mostly he doesn't."

"Oh, God. So . . . what's her name?" and Rowan knew she was right, she knew it wasn't a wild guess, she knew there was someone else going for pizza the nights he was out of town. Half the nights of the week.

"I didn't bother trying to find out. That part of it isn't any of my business. This," she tapped the photocopies of the months and years of unpaid child support, "this is my business and nothing else."

Rowan didn't believe things could happen so fast. She stood at the bedroom doorway watching Sue look in Jim's drawers, find the bankbook and the chequebook and copy the numbers onto a piece of paper. She supposed she was probably being disloyal or something, but she was damned if she was going to get into this mess any deeper than she was already in it. If Sue wanted to go through the goddamn drawers, let her, it was no skin off Rowan's nose.

Four hours later, Sue phoned. "So," she said happily, "it's done. All I had to do was go to the court house and talk to the clerk. She made some notes and went down the hall and came back five minutes later with this signed paper, and we went down another hall to the sheriff's office and she handed it to him and he read it and grinned and headed off to the parking lot. Cost me ten dollars."

"What did you do?"

"Garnisheed his wages. I'd'a seized his bank accounts, too, but there was bugger nothing in them. He's going to be in one helluva mood when he finds out, you'd better be ready for it."

"Oh, I'm ready." Rowan looked over at the stack of cardboard boxes piled on the porch. "If you hear someone banging at your door about midnight, don't be scared, it'll just be me tryin' to get in out of the noise!"

But there wasn't any noise. He knew as soon as he saw the boxes what they meant. He just stared up at her, and she hoped his stomach hurt as much as hers did.

"Sue was over," she said quietly. "With photocopies from Family Court."

"Fuckin' bitch," he breathed bitterly. "I can explain."

"You've lied to me all along." She knew she sounded amazed and disbelieving. "From the very beginning you've just lied and bullshitted and lied some more. And if there is one thing I can't find a lot of use for it's a liar. I'd like you to give me back the spare key, please."

"Just like that?"

"Just like that."

She waited until he had packed the boxes in the pickup and locked the canopy door, she waited until he got in his truck, fired up the engine and drove off. She waited until the sound of the motor faded and then she waited some more. Finally, she closed the door, very gently, and locked it, then went to bed and lay there in the dark staring at nothing at all. Funny, for something that was none of her business, it sure did hurt. Hurt so bad she couldn't even cry.

Rowan went to work, did her shift, smiled and chatted with the other ferry frantics, told nobody she had shown Jim the door, and felt like shit on a stick the whole time. Three days later she felt so wretched she phoned in to say she couldn't go to work. No sooner had she hung up the phone than her body decided there was no way she was going to be

112   *Anne Cameron*

a liar. Her belly knotted with cramps, her throat tightened, nausea made her dizzy and she hurried to the jane. She spent most of her day there, trying to empty her brain by way of her bowel.

The next day she gave up trying to be brave and stalwart and handle it all on her own, and she went in to the medical clinic. The doctor told her she probably had the flu. "There's a lot of it going around," she said with a wan smile.

"Physician, heal thyself," Rowan guessed.

"Take these." The tired-looking woman brought a package of samples from a drawer in her desk. "They've worked better than anything else I've tried. At least the head stops pounding and your eyes don't try to jump out of your face each time you move. And these," she brought out another small package, "will at least keep your guts in your body. Plenty of juice and other fluids, go to bed if you can, and just keep repeating, It could be worse, It could be worse."

"Right," Rowan nodded, "and the first thing you know it *will* be worse!"

"Spot on. If you don't feel better in four days, come back and see me again."

Two days later Rowan felt better, and the third day she was back at work, and she could do it. But she was still pale, still empty, still feeling like shit on a stick.

Jim wasn't there and yet he was everywhere. She couldn't let the weeds ruin the garden, that was too much like cutting off your nose to spite your face, so she went out with a hoe and hacked disinterestedly between the tidy rows. Each evening she made sure she remembered to go out and turn on the trickle irrigation, each morning she forced herself to remember to go back and turn it off again. The garden went nuts and when Megan dropped by to make sure Rowan was doing okay on her own, although she tactfully didn't say that was why she had dropped by, she suggested Rowan should think of quitting her job and just growing food. "You're doing something right," she laughed. Rowan privately figured what she was doing right was leaving the whole thing as much to itself as possible. It looked like a jungle. But the salads were delicious. She couldn't cut the leaf lettuce as fast as it grew back. Then she had to pick what seemed like a washtub load of bush beans and another washtub load of scarlet runner beans. Zucchini tried to take over the world, vegetable marrow shoved against the fence, the corn filled out and the tomatoes demanded to be picked.

"I'm going to smother in all that stuff," she said, "and I haven't got a clue what to do with it. Maybe I'll take it to the food bank or something."

"Bring it here," Sue said idly, "I've got a basement full of jars and all the time in the world right now."

"How come?"

"Why," Sue laughed bitterly, "it's my unscheduled unwanted holiday, the one they call 'layoff', the one that gives me pogey, which is a fraction of what was barely a living wage in the first place."

"You going anywhere?"

"Yeah. Of course. Prince Charles is coming by after lunch and we're going to the Riviera for a few days."

"Right. Sorry, that was stupid of me."

"So put on the coffee, I'll come over and help you pick stuff." She started laughing. "It's funny, eh, here we are, and the only reason we know each other has been sent off down the road, and there we'll be, harvesting his fucking garden!"

It was funny, but not exactly funny ha-ha, more like funny-gross, or funny-yuck, but they made themselves smile and they picked everything that even hinted at being ripe. Sue took the boxes home and a few days later phoned to say the pickles, chutney, salsa, and whatever else she had invented was in jars. "I can bring it over any time, or you can come and get it."

"Can you hang onto it for a while?"

"Sure. Why?"

"I'm putting the house up for sale."

"Christ almighty," was all Sue said.

It wasn't only that Jim seemed to be lurking just out of sight everywhere she went. It wasn't just that the place seemed hollow and mocking or that she hadn't managed to pack all of his stuff and kept coming across things like his screwdriver set or his tackle box. Just about every emotional upheaval she had ever had was linked in her mind and soul to moving. Good or bad, happy or sad, when something had happened, she'd packed her gear and changed her surroundings. Even if she couldn't have put the feeling into words, she could put it into actions. She phoned the real estate agent and started packing.

It didn't happen overnight, but it happened. She found a new place, she got the papers, her old place sold for far more than she had dared hope and she signed everything and moved into the new place. When people asked her what her new house was like, Rowan grinned. "Oh," she said, "it's one of those places where the taps run all the time and the drains never do." Everyone knew what she meant, because everyone had lived in a place like that one or more times.

"It's a bit big for one person, isn't it?" Sue dared.

"Yeah, I guess it is, but you know how it is, no matter how much room you've got, you fill it up with junk."

"Why'd you get a place so big?"

"I like the yard," Rowan shrugged.

The yard was huge, three times the size of most municipal lots, with enormous walnut trees growing along the back fence. The lilac bushes were taller than she was and the two huge rhododendrons in the front yard promised to make springtime a glory of bloom and colour. If Rowan paid attention to where she was looking she could avoid the sight of the pulp mill stacks with smoke pouring up from them, forming a column of carcinogenic crud that looked like the pictures of the mushroom clouds over Hiroshima and Nagasaki. The front walk was flanked with flowers, the front fence was hidden in a riot of roses and the apple trees in the side yard were loaded.

"Jesus," Justin breathed, "you're gonna spend all your spare time just mowing this grass." He poked her gently in the ribs. "Get a ride-on mower and I'll do it for you once a week for only, oh, ten bucks."

"Five." She poked him back. "After all, you'd get a free ride."

"There you go," he shook his head, "you've got a deal. Providing I can use the ride-on to do Mom's lawn. Which," he frowned at his mother, "I wind up doing for zip-all."

"Which," Sue corrected, "you wind up doing in return for a place to sleep, food to eat, and clean jeans just about any time you want to take the time and trouble to do the laundry."

"There's no winning with that woman," he decided. "She could argue a coon out of an apple tree." He squinted up into the branches. "Speaking of which..."

"Split 'em with you," Rowan bargained. "You pick 'em and I'll take half."

"Those aren't eating apples," Sue corrected, "so if you're going to do anything with them you have to either freeze them or..."

"Tell you what," Rowan teased, "you do with my half what you do with your half and you can keep half of my half."

"Stuff it," Sue offered. "You help."

"I don't know anything at all about canning! My grandma did that stuff."

"So? You won't learn any younger, right?"

Applesauce weekend is one of those ghastly times that live forever in memory. Alys picked, Tiffany picked, Justin picked, Sue and Rowan peeled, cored, cooked, strained, bottled, capped and glared at the boxes of apples still to be done.

"Why does the church make such a big deal out of the loaves and fishes routine?" Tiffany asked, rummaging through Sue's crates of canning supplies. "Seems to me it's the jars and lids would be the real miracle! How come every time we open a jar of preserves there's this flat cap we throw away and then there's this screw-lid thing we put in this damn box, but come time to live through this canning nightmare there's always more jars than there are screw-lids? You'd think there'd be more screw-lids because they don't break and the goddamn jars *do*!"

"Stop swearing," Sue chided casually. "It sounds like hell."

"Can I take some of these apples over to Mrs. Figuero?" Justin asked. "She's a friend as well as a customer, okay?"

"Jesus, take a truckload," Rowan groused. "How much applesauce can a human being eat, anyway?"

"Sell 'em, why don't you?" Tiffany blurted. "And make a dollar or two."

"Off you go, Miz Trump." Rowan flexed her hands. "Just don't forget to file your income tax return, okay?"

"Me too!" Alys decided.

"Finish the jars-and-rings miracle first," Sue corrected. "And find out from Rowan how much of what you make selling *her* apples you have to hand over to her."

"Tell you what," Rowan said, tossing her paring knife onto the pile of peelings at her feet. "I'll give you a dime if you can sell the whole friggin' lot."

"Thank the good lord," Sue breathed. "I thought we'd be here until Wednesday."

"Wow!" The kids were gone, down the back steps, along the walk, through the back gate, and into the alley, spreading out with a few samples in their hands to try to flog the surplus to the neighbours.

"Let's clean up this kitchen and call it a day." Rowan shook her head. "A weekend, more like it. We've got applesauce till hell won't hold it. We'll be eating the goddamn stuff three years from now!"

Somehow you never get a kick in the teeth without getting a kick in the face, too. Rowan came home from early shift to find Sue waiting for her with a face almost as long as her leg. "You've got some bad news coming to you," Sue warned.

"I'd rather have good news," Rowan sighed, "it's rarer."

"Yeah, well, get ready for it."

Never the brightest dog in the world, Lucky Lou had decided to jump the fence and take a tour of the neighbourhood. She made it over the fence but was so excited by her acrobatic ability she tore down the alley at full speed, and tried to cross the street. She got halfway across and though the truck driver hit his brakes and did everything he could, Lucky Lou's luck ran out and she was dead before the huge machine came to a halt.

"One of the neighbours phoned me." Sue handed Rowan a roll of toilet paper. "She had seen Justin doing your lawn so she knew I knew you. Or at least knew *he* knew you. "

"Where is she?"

"In the shed. Justin said he'd dig the grave for you, but he didn't know where you'd want it."

"Under a chestnut tree, I guess," and then Rowan excused herself, went to the bathroom and sobbed bitterly. Lucky Lou hadn't been much of a dog, and she hadn't had time to be scared or to suffer, but Rowan couldn't help feeling guilty. If she'd stayed out of town, there'd have been no oil truck and Lucky Lou wouldn't have been hit by it. Of course, there were logging trucks, gravel trucks, pickup trucks, and mindlessness can always find a way to impact with the grill of some kind of vehicle.

She didn't sob when Jim showed up at the new place. She didn't invite him inside, either. She stepped out onto the back porch and stood, arms crossed, hands clenched into tight fists.

"What do you want?" she demanded.

"Usually people start off by saying hello, how are you," he said tightly.

"Usually people don't visit people who don't want to be visited."

"I left some stuff behind when I moved."

"It's in the shed, two cardboard boxes, right by the back door, with your name marked on the lid. Goodbye."

"I was hoping this could be done without any kind of fight," he glared, "but I guess I was wrong. So here it is short and sweet. I figure you owe me something."

She laughed harshly. "I figure about all I owe you is a goddamn good kick in the ass, so if you want to collect that, just turn around, bend over, grab your ankles and take a deep breath."

"You sold our place," he accused.

"Our place? *Our*? Reach out and grab a world, fella, maybe you'll catch hold of some reality at the same time. Who do you think you are? The Canadian beaver? The one builds his home with his tail?"

"Oh, the west coast barroom wit is at it again."

"Yeah. And the west coast barroom wit is just about ready to get at something else, too. Like phoning the bikers to see if they want to make a hundred dollars getting garbage off my fuckin' steps!"

"You got a better price for that place because of the garden and the work I put in than you'd'a got the way it was when I moved there," he shouted.

"Yeah? Well, just put it down to what it didn't cost you for rent." She shook her head wonderingly. "You really do take the cake, so help me God."

"And that's your answer?"

"No, it's not an answer," she said, turning to go back into the house. "I wouldn't justify your goddamn stupid question with an answer."

"Cheap bitch," he breathed.

"I must have been, to hang out with a two-bit turd like you." She closed the door, locked it and pulled the curtain across the small window. If only that was all a person had to do to close out the effects and memories of times once sweet and now gone sour. All that fun, all that laughter, all that closeness, and the knowledge it hadn't been sincere turned it to compost, a woman she didn't even know had been there for most of it, invisible, and unacknowledged, but changing everything.

After a moment or two, she heard him go down the steps. When she knew he was gone she whirled and pounded her hands on the countertop. "Damn, damn, damn!" she shouted, "Damn, damn, *damn*!"

There was no doubt the house was too big for one person and one dog. Rowan used only a fraction of the space. The kitchen was enormous and even with a big table and six chairs in it, there was something stark about the bare counters, the expanse of floor. A pipe band could have practised marching manoeuvres in the living room, and in what had originally been a dining room, you could feed a Shriners convention. The downstairs bathroom had a toilet, an old pedestal wash basin which Rowan loved, and a tub supported by thick legs ending in claw feet, a tub long enough for her to lie down in water up to her chin. And enough empty floor space to allow three couples to swirl and dip in a ballroom dancing display. Her downstairs bedroom was at least as big as the living room, with big old windows that started a foot from the floor and went up almost to the ceiling. Wide stairs went up to the three bedrooms, bathroom and hallway on the second floor, and in the ceiling of the hallway was a little square you could push aside to gain access to the attic.

"It looks," Rowan confessed, "like the local coven meets there."

"What do you care, as long as they're quiet?"

"Oh, they're quiet all right. There's so much empty space in this house you could turn the television on full bore and not hear it at the other end of the hallway. I feel like I'm rattling in here. I don't know what I was thinking of when I bought it. Or maybe I wasn't thinking."

"Don't complain." Sue cut slices from the cake she had brought with her. "It could be worse, you could be curled up in a ball trying to live in your own back pocket."

"I must have had my head in a jar when I bought this place. I bought it because I liked the big yard, and didn't stop to realize there's more room inside the house than there is outside!"

"I'd trade you in a minute," Sue sighed. "You've got a basement. I'd commit obscenities for a basement. Except we're so jammed in that place there's no room for really inventive obscenities! I knew it was too small when we bought it, but what else could we afford? And anyway You Know Who had more plans than there are sea-lice on a rock cod. It pisses me off! I can barely scrape up the damned mortgage payments let alone put money aside for taxes, and we're living in each other's pockets, with no chance of adding on a room or two. Unless we win the 6/49."

"You'll get ahead of it."

"Not likely," Sue shook her head. "I haven't even managed to pay off the interest on the mortgage. Until I do that, I'm not making any dent in what I owe."

"You're kidding."

"Nope. So don't complain to me about too much space, kiddo. I'd give my eye teeth for even just a little bit."

"Well, I'm not switching places with you," Rowan laughed. "The thought of packing stuff in boxes again makes my skin creep. So if you want space you'll have to kick out the coven and move into that damned creepy attic."

"Twist my rubber arm." Sue tasted her cake, nodded once and wiggled her fork at Rowan. "C'mon, eat up, find out what it is gets done with that applesauce. Incidentally, what do you do with yours?"

"I'm saving it," Rowan admitted, "just in case there's a famine or something."

"Make applesauce cake."

"I don't bake. I've got all I can do to cook meals. My grandma was so good at baking, it seemed only fair to let her shine, and I just concentrated on eating it up so she had a reason to bake some more."

"I love baking."

"Good. I love eating it."

"All the best magazines say it's eating cakes and muffins and cookies and stuff like that puts pounds on your hips and spare tires on your waist. If they ever see you they'll have to revise their entire marketing strategy. I don't think I've ever seen anyone eat as much as you do and not gain weight."

"What it is," Rowan said, dabbing cream on her cake, "is I eat so much I lose weight packing it all around. And then, of course, there's my strict exercise regime. My television doesn't have a remote control, I have to get up out of my chair and walk over to change channels."

They moved on to other topics of conversation, but something was noodling in Rowan's head. A few days later she brought it up and put it out on the table. Sue hesitated, said she would think about it, and they both let it drop until next time.

"I went to see the family court," Sue said abruptly, "and if you're serious about it, I can do it."

"What?"

"Evict the coven," Sue grinned. "He's so far behind in support payments that any equity he thinks he has in the house can be declared forfeit by the court."

He showed up just before Christmas, but not to see Rowan. Sue let him in and gestured to a chair at the kitchen table. He sat down, looking around as if he were interested in buying the place. "Nice tree," he nodded approval.

"Yes," Sue said with no expression in her voice at all, "but I'm sure you didn't come here to see the Christmas decorations."

"That's right. I came because I think your lawyer and my lawyer are both full of crap."

"They may well be." Sue poured two cups of coffee, set one in front of Jim and one at her own place, then got the cream and sugar and put them in the middle of the table like a fortified wall.

"How much did you get for the house?"

"That's none of your business."

"Don't give me that horseshit! That was my house, too!"

"You signed away any interest you might have had in the house, remember? You signed it all away when I hit you for back maintenance. That's how you got out of paying what you owed me and the kids."

"Then how come I still have the goddamn court hanging over my head?"

"Because the back maintenance was for what you owed in the past and what's hanging over your head is what you owe for the future. Don't be so goddamn stupid, Jim, you know full well how things stand."

"So how much did you get for the house?"

"That's none of your business."

"I figure you got enough that you should let me off the hook on maintenance, that's what I figure."

"You figure wrong."

"Listen." He stirred his coffee slowly. "Let's stop this, okay? I'll stop being proddy and you'll stop being shirty and we'll talk reasonably for a change, okay? What it is, is this. Lorene has got four kids, okay, and her ex doesn't pay child support. She's been on welfare for a couple of years but if I'm working and living there the welfare thing starts to get sticky. So that's gonna mean that I'll be supporting two adults and four kids. . . five in a few months," he grinned proudly, and waited to see if Sue was going to congratulate him. She didn't. "So, what I thought was this. There won't be any hassle about you selling the house, okay? And there won't be any hassle about me paying maintenance. I figure you got a good pocketful for the place, and half of that, by rights, should be mine, but I'll give it to you as a lump sum payoff on the child support. What do you say?"

"Drink your coffee and leave," Sue smiled sweetly. "There was a big mortgage still on that place, which you seem to have conveniently forgotten. That had to be paid off before anything else got done. What was left wasn't exactly enough to make you look like Daddy Warbucks, okay? And the court looked at all the paperwork, took into account the fact I was the only one making payments on the place, paying the taxes, getting the roof fixed and all that good shit, then looked at the B.S. you've been pulling for the past five years and wrote you right out of the picture. And you signed, Jim. It got you off the hook, remember? You are oh-yew-tee. Except for the child support, which is supposed to come on the fifteenth of every month, without fail. And which *will* come or we'll be back to the part where I get the garnishee and you get the warning that your assets can be seized."

"Jesus Christ, Suzy, what do you think? I'm made of money or something? I've got a kid on the way. Why does that kid have to live like a churchmouse just because you're a vindictive twat?"

"Let's put this in terms even an asshole like you can understand, okay? I couldn't go into a Ford dealer and get a brand new car, make two payments on it and then park it in the garage, go down to the Chev dealer and buy another new car and decide not to finish paying for the Ford, but keep it in my driveway all the same. They'd come and tow it away. Just because you've decided to have a fourth kid is no reason the first three should starve in a ditch. You knew they existed, you knew you had payments, you knew the court was not amused by your bullshit, and you couldn't keep your pants buttoned. So you pay."

"Jesus." He shook his head. "You didn't use to be like this."

"That's right, I didn't," she agreed, "but I am now."

"So I get slid out of my fair share," he said, sounding so much like a pouting kid Sue nearly laughed. But the laughter couldn't make it past the cold fury in her chest.

"It's more like you screwed yourself out of everything."

That's when Rowan came home from a day out in her rowboat, walked in the back door and nearly bumped into Jim as he shoved his chair back from the table and prepared to stand shouting and roaring down at Sue, still in her seat. Instead, he looked at Rowan, then looked at Sue, and sneered. "Ah," he mocked, "I get it. A couple of real queerie-dearies, aren't you?"

"Who *is* this asshole?" Rowan asked.

"Some yutz." Sue was pale with fury but forced a smile that wouldn't have fooled anyone. "Seems the world has been grossly unfair to the poor little fucker and he came here hoping for charity."

"Fuck the two of yous," Jim yelled.

"Well, actually," Rowan laughed and meant it, "you did. But you won't do it again, not one way or the other. Don't come back, okay?"

"What a hoot!" He was shaking with fury. "What a fuckin' hoot. Two of them, and they both steal *my* money and wind up livin' together. What a joke."

He left, slamming the door and yelling at Babe to get the hell out of his way before he kicked her in the head. Rowan opened the back door, snapped her fingers, and old Babe waddled into the kitchen, whining.

"Oh, don't get your fur in a knot," Rowan soothed, "it's just a temporary windstorm. Kind of like a perambulating fart passing through the intestines of life."

"A bit more substantial than a fart," Sue corrected. "But not much more."

Rowan took her gunny sack of cod to the sink and went for her filleting knives. She stropped them carefully on her bone-handled steel, then pulled the cutting board from under the sink. Nothing else got cut with her knives, and nothing but fish got cut on the board. Even the kids were careful about it. None of them wanted to endure Rowan's fury if her knives were interfered with, and nobody wanted fish-tasting sandwiches.

"You want these for supper or you want them in the freezer?" she asked, as if nothing had been coming down when she came in the door.

"What do you think?" Sue sniffed, her anger coming out in tears.

"Someone told me once that people who answer a question with another question get lumps on their heads," Rowan smiled, glad her own connections with the dipper had ended and there weren't three living, breathing, eternally hungry tendrils still clinging and strangling.

Sue stared at Rowan, looked away, then looked back. Rowan just kept smiling and filleting. "I think we should have them for supper," Sue decided. "I think we should have them with mashed potatoes. And

I think I'll mash the potatoes myself. And with each mash try to convince myself it's his head!"

"I love whipped potatoes."

What Jim had yelled wasn't true when he yelled it, but by Easter his accusation was no longer unfounded. Rowan and Sue were more than just joint owners, more than tenants in common, and what had been Sue's bedroom became the TV room, over the objections of Alys who thought it grossly unfair she should share a room with Tiffany while Justin had a room all to himself. "Oh, do shut up," Sue said easily. "You're almost fifteen years old, for God's sake, and you still whine like a three-year-old."

Alys stalked out of the room as if it were beneath her dignity to even associate with them.

"My eye," Rowan said wearily. "I don't know how many real uproars Peter Pan and I had because of these kids. I spent more time trying not to be involved with them than I spent shining my shoes or ironing my clothes! I didn't even want them to visit, and now I live with them."

"I know what you mean," Sue agreed. "Many's the time, believe me, I don't want to have to visit with them, either."

"It was a good instinct. I felt kind of mean about it at the time but the more I'm around them the more I know it was a real survival instinct."

"You should have paid more attention to it," Sue laughed softly. "There really are times when the only consolation I have is that they will leave home one day."

"Not soon enough!"

"Why'd you dig in your heels so much with him?"

"I think I was afraid they'd come to visit him and I'm the one would be stuck trying to deal with them."

"And here you are, stuck with trying to deal with them."

"Yeah. And it ain't funny, McGee," she said, before they both burst out laughing. They sat on the sofa together, shoulders touching, Rowan half leaning against Sue, her head almost but not quite on Sue's shoulder. "I think maybe," she said softly, "part of it was I never saw him with them, so I had no reason to think he ever did anything about them, or to them, or with them. Except talk and get upset. And you, well, even before I saw you or knew you I knew you looked after them. I don't want to put myself in any kind of position where I'm *stuck* with them." Sue nodded, but Rowan felt impelled to try to explain more clearly. "Maybe I've got a thing about not being involved."

"Maybe." Sue's voice was gentle, laughter bubbling just under the surface of the word.

"I mean, yeah, I'm involved with you but I don't have to. . .I don't have to *do* it all. Make it happen. Invent the world every morning. If I felt I had to, I could just saunter off, free and clear. And I like it that way. I like to feel I choose to be here, choose to stay."

Justin got a job after school, on weekends and holidays carrying bundles for a roofing company. He came home pale with exhaustion and more than once fell asleep in the bathtub. He joked constantly, making puns, playing with words, teasing gently. Acquaintances thought he was a real fun guy, but often, especially when he didn't know anybody was looking at him, a sadness would come into his eyes, and more than once Rowan thought of the pound puppies, deprived of litter mates, separated from their mothers, sitting staring at the gate, not even knowing for sure what it was they were hoping to see.

"Ah, the fuckers." Justin shook his head. "I almost admire them. Because I'm a student the labour laws have exceptions, right? So they say they're paying me six bucks an hour, but that's not what I get paid. I don't get any lunch time, I don't get coffee break time, none of that. And they've taken the six bucks an hour a step further. There's maybe three guys up on the roof, right, with bundles of shingles spread out where they can get at them easily, just lay 'em, fit 'em, and whap 'em in place, zip-zip-zip. And I'm the asshole has to hump those bundles from the back of the truck, up the ladder, to where they can get at 'em, eh. So I haul oh, I don't know, say five or ten of those bundles one after the other, zippedy-doo-dah because we're all in a rush, eh, and the fuckers are heavy. I mean heavy! And dead weight. That's a strange thing, you know, like a sack of feed is fifty pounds and that's fifty pounds but a fifty-pound sack'a'cement seems heavier. It's smaller, I guess, and just. . .I don't know. A bundle of shingles is heavy. And takin' it up a ladder, well, it's heavier each rung up you go because there's only this little part of your foot takin' the weight on the ladder rung. So I haul say ten bundles up to the roof, and if it's like a warehouse or something I'm running spreading bundles where the roofers can get 'em, and just about the time I'm ready to fall on my fuckin' face they're set for fifteen minutes and I go for a drinka water or something and then catch m'breath. And I don't get paid except when I'm humpin' bundles! So they say it's six bucks an hour but what it works out to is more like three-fifty or four bucks an hour and I have to tell you it makes me want to get a pair of those rubber thong sandals and one of them goddamn coolie hats!" He forced his smile. "You wannee rickshaw, rady?"

"Stay in school, Justin," Rowan said softly. "Baffle 'em with brains, not with footwork."

"Yeah?" he shrugged. "You know somethin', Rowan, it's a damn fine idea. And who knows, in other circumstances I'd maybe do 'er. But somehow I can't see me paying room and board in the city, plus food, plus clothes, plus shoes, plus transportation, plus tuition, plus books and doin' all that homework as well as racin' up and down a goddamn ladder with a load on my back!"

"I've got money." She didn't look at him, she just stared at the pattern of the carpet. "And what in hell is money for if not to spend. Go to school, and stop worrying about what doesn't matter."

"But it does." And she knew there would be no changing his mind. "I'm tired of spongin', Rowan. Can you understand that? I know you're payin' more'n your share of things around here."

"You might know it," Rowan smiled, then looked at him, met his even gaze. "But that doesn't mean it's any of your business, right? Anything I'm doing, I'm doing because I want to do it."

"Whoever's business it is," Justin smiled gently, "I still know it. Okay, I'm bushed, and I admit it. I bet my mom has felt like this just about every night for the past three or four years. So what am I complainin' about, eh? And what you say about school makes sense, probably. I'm just tired. And I'm tired of being tired!"

"Just think about it, please. Life can be a right bitch at times." But she knew Justin liked things easy, and it was easier to settle for what was immediately at hand than to go out and scrabble like hell in the hope you might, with a lot of luck, get something a little bit more. Or maybe he was just being realistic. "Who can tell," she asked Sue that night in bed, as they snuggled together comfortably, "what is achievement, what is overachievement and what is underachievement?"

"I don't know," Sue yawned.

"I don't either."

Alys got Justin's room when he left home and went to work on a construction crew, putting condo developments on what had once been a working farm just above the high-tide line. The old orchard was chain-sawed out, the split-rail fences were hauled away and burned, the weathered barn and outbuildings were shoved over by massive bulldozers and once the fires were out, the condos appeared like mushrooms after the rain. The full-timers sighed, some shook their heads sadly, but it was all legal, in spite of the Agricultural Land Reserve, and anyway, they were told, you can't stand in the way of progress.

When the condo development was done, the crew moved on to another lovely little bay, and started on another development. When that was done, they had two months of what Justin called "hiatus" and then went to a small island where a very clever individual had bought four farms, then applied to build a private golf course. Of course, the members needed someplace to stay between rounds of golf, so a hotel had to be built, and some of the members had children who, as we all know, do not do well in hotels, so another condo development had to be built. Bit by bit the coast was being carved up like a pie, with the best pieces reserved for the wealthy and the rock and scrub left for those who would become the chambermaids and gas jockeys serving the favoured.

During the election campaign for Regional Board, one of the candidates talked so fluently and with such apparent heartfelt sincerity about saving the unique way of life and protecting the priceless heritage of the coast, he was elected chairman by what the local newspaper called a landslide. Everyone expected the permit applications to be frozen and stringent new guidelines to be introduced. The first year the knight in shining armour was in office, a record number of development permits were approved by the Regional Board. The voters sighed wearily and promised themselves things would be different come next election. One wit sent a carton of toilet paper to the Regional Board, and though there was no note, everyone knew the idea was the shits could divide it up among themselves, the way they were dividing up the under-the-table payoffs. The former chairman, the one defeated by a landslide, got a job as advisor to the fish farmers' association. What he knew about farming fish could have been poked in his eye without interfering with his vision, but it wasn't that expertise got him his job anyway.

Alys was pregnant by the time she was sixteen, and flatly refused to even consider putting the child up for adoption. "I don't see why you're being so mean about it," she griped. "How much space can a little thing take up, anyway? She or he could share my room."

"Great," Rowan growled, "but who's going to look after her while you're in school?"

"I'm not going back to school! I hate school! A baby needs its mom to be *with* it, not in school!"

"And who's going to feed this little bundle of joy? Who's going to buy all the boots and shoes and jeans and sweaters?" Sue asked coldly.

"Well, gee whiz!" Alys wept. "If you won't even help me out, I guess I can go to the welfare." And she waited for her mother to reject the idea totally. When Sue didn't, Alys glared. "Maybe if you hadn't worked all the time . . ." she began.

Sue exploded. "Oh no you don't! I'm not wearing that one! Everybody works, kid, and in spite of what you see and believe on TV, everybody always has. If you used your brain instead of just letting it fester inside your thick bonehead, you'd find out that only the wealthy have ever had the option of staying home full-time with their kids!"

"See? See how you are?" Alys wailed, and pelted up the stairs, sobbing bitterly.

The silence stretched. Tif very wisely picked up her homework and vanished, leaving Sue and Rowan alone in the huge living room. After long minutes of strained silence, Sue spoke, her voice uneven. "I don't care if you think I'm being unreasonable," she said. "I know what would happen and I've done about all the diaper changing I'm interested in doing."

"Amen," Rowan agreed.

Sue stared, then relaxed visibly, got up off the sofa and moved to where Rowan sat in the big overstuffed chair. Sue sat on Rowan's knee and leaned against her with her face in the curve of Rowan's neck. "I was worried you'd want . . ."

"Me?" Rowan laughed softly. "Hey, I don't even want 'em when they're *big*, let alone when they're small!"

Alys wanted someone who would love her unconditionally. From *The Waltons* on TV, she had picked up the idea that a baby was the way to get what she wanted. When Brittany learned to say "no" before she was two years old, Alys was crushed. She responded to it by getting pregnant again. Maybe the next kid would be a TV kid and never rebel, never say no, never be as ornery as Alys herself had always been.

Tiffany, who had been painted as passive aggressive, just watched the unfolding of the installments, and shook her head each time Justin moved on to another job, another town, another party, another big meaningful relationship, and Alys moved from romantic involvement to romantic involvement.

The boyfriends checked in and the boyfriends checked out. Some of them made a regular habit of passing out, which didn't hasten their departure any. Alys rented whatever she could find and lived on welfare, and the boyfriends contributed greater or lesser amounts depending on their temperaments, jobs, and sobriety levels. Each of them seemed more or less the same as any of the others as far as Rowan was concerned, but, she told herself, who was she to judge? After all, she'd been a lot older than Alys when she'd jumped out of the frying pan and into the fire, and look what a good job she'd done of picking the dry teat. The kid would just have to learn that the guy on the white horse wasn't going to canter down the street and into her life.

"You have to find a way to provide for yourself the things you need in life," she tried.

"Oh, sure," Alys sighed. "Sure, Rowan, tell me all about it. What would you know about anything like that? The way you live, I mean. It isn't exactly normal, is it?"

"Seems pretty normal to me. Who's to say what's normal and what's not? I wasn't talking normal, anyway, I was telling you that nobody but you can be the one you depend on for the things you need. Make a list, Allie, and write down what it was about each one that sucked you into thinking it was Prince Charming time, then figure out what you got out of it."

"You're wrong," Alys sniffed, "and that's all there is to it."

"Jesus," Rowan told Sue, "it's like talking to a bucket of water!"

Justin moved in with a woman six years older than he was, with two kids by two different men. "Oh, you know how it is," he joked, "I grew up with an older woman, I got imprinted on older women, it's only natural I'd fall for an older woman. Anyway, if it was the other way around and I was six years older than her, nobody would even notice. Shouldn't equality work both ways?"

"Sure, guy, sure," Sue forced a smile. "And I guess if my sex life is none of your business, yours is none of mine."

"That's my girl," he smiled. "Just wait'll you meet the kids, you'll love them the minute you see them. Great kids."

"I'm sure." Sue nodded, she even smiled, but not even Justin could pretend she was drooling with eagerness. Still, she marked the calendar with the birthdates of the kids and made sure the cards and presents got mailed in time. Within a few months, the kids were talking to her on the phone, calling her Nanna, and every now and again a big brown envelope would arrive with kindergarten scribblings and grade-one alphabet copying. "I think I understand," she told Rowan, "what it was had you recoiling and leaping backward when His Royal Self started hinting that you should be ready to fall on your face with gratitude for the chance to get to know my kids."

"Yeah," Rowan nodded. She put her finger on the string as she tied shut the box of socks and underwear Sue was readying for the mail. "It's like living at the wrong end of the vacuum cleaner hose. No matter how deep you dig in your fingernails, bit by bit by bit you get sucked in."

By the time Alys was twenty-two, she had three kids by three different men and was living in a rented unit in a mustard-yellow apartment complex swarming with kids. Once a month Rowan gritted her teeth, made herself smile determinedly, and cooked chicken until she thought there wouldn't be a living hen in a four-day ride, and Alys and her kids ate Sunday dinner at Grandma's house, with mountains of mashed potatoes and gallons of buttered carrots. Sometimes, during the meal, Rowan would look around the table and stifle the guffaws trying to burst from her belly. She who had never wanted anything to do with kids was up to her ears in them. Brittany, Tyler and Brandi grinned and chewed, grinned and swallowed, grinned and reached for more, and Alys picked at her food briefly, then smoked one cigarette after another while watching everyone else eat. When Sue complained of the smoke, Alys sighed like a martyr viewing the bonfire for the first time, left the table and sat on the sofa smoking, sighing and watching.

"How do you keep so calm and quiet?" Sue asked Rowan in bed after one of the interminable sabbath dinners.

"I just remind myself that none of it has anything to do with me," Rowan said. "It's only four or five hours a month, and it's no worse than any eight-and-a-half-hour shift in tourist season."

"I wish she'd drown in the gravy," Sue confessed. "She seems to think someone stole something from her, so the world owes her. . .everything. If she could arrange it, I bet she'd have someone breathe in and out for her."

"If I could arrange it I'd make it happen," Rowan agreed, "then bribe that person to pull a wildcat strike and let Alys smother."

"I feel so awful." Sue was suddenly sobbing, gripping the edge of the sheet and trembling. Rowan pulled her close, stroking her back, feeling the hot tears trickle down her own skin. "Any one of those kids is nicer than Alys ever was, and yet I look at them and all I feel is an incredible dose of boredom! And what's ahead for them? She doesn't read stories to them, she doesn't play with them, she doesn't do anything about alphabet games or let's pretend or . . . they seem to live with the TV implanted in their belly buttons."

"I don't remember anybody reading me any stories," Rowan said softly, "and I'm not saying it did me any good, and I'm not saying it didn't do me harm, but . . . I'm doing okay."

"You're tough," Sue sniffled, then wiped her eyes with the pillow slip. "But they aren't."

"I wasn't tough when I was their age," Rowan laughed. "I was scared stiff and going from one foster home to another."

"But you had your grandma!"

"Yeah, and they have you."

"I'm not half the woman your grandma was."

Rowan thought for a long time, then shook her head. "My grandma was probably not half the woman you are," she decided. "I adored her, but things that didn't make any sense to me at the time make some sense now, and things I thought were just the way everyone's life was, now look a lot different. My grandma was a Bunkhouse Bertha. Did such a great job on her own kid that she took off and what she did makes Alys look like Snow White. For years I thought my grandma got her float camp cook jobs because she was the greatest cook in the world, but we'd be shut down for snow or something and we'd wind up in town for a few months, then she'd hear something from someone and she'd get all gussied up. 'Put on my war paint,' she'd say. She'd go to the bar for a few nights and . . . she'd get a job." Rowan made herself shrug as if none of it had any sting in it. "The mind rebels," she said mockingly, "at the thought of what the application form looked like."

"But . . ."

"Yeah, she was still the greatest grandma the world has ever known, and she saved my ass. But I bet the good people of a half a dozen towns sighed and said, Oh my, I wonder what her granddaughter will come to. . ."

Tiffany finished high school, then sat down at the kitchen table with both her mothers and quietly stated her peace. "And because I'm coming in from out of town, and because I've got really good marks, I can live in residence. This is how much it will cost." She pointed to a figure on the sheet of paper. "And this is how much per year I can get as a student loan. And this is what I think I can get by on for groceries."

"Where's the column for entertainment, medicine, medical plan and incidentals?" Rowan interrupted.

Tiffany bit her lip and shook her head sharply, then took a deep breath. "I think I can get a job," she said hesitantly, "and I think what I get at the job will cover all that. I just don't know where I'll get that job."

"And transportation?"

"If I'm living in residence, I'll be right there. I won't need transportation."

"You can't stay in residence all the time. What about the job? Getting to it and from it? What about coming home once in a while so we don't forget what you look like?"

Tif's eyes brimmed, and she took another of those deep breaths that hurt the two listening to her. "I don't know," she admitted. "There's all this stuff that I just can't know about until it happens."

"Register," Sue said suddenly. "Just register, darling. Get your loan, get into residence if you can. Do what needs done. We'll find the money somewhere. Who knows," she sobbed suddenly, "maybe we can sell applesauce!"

Every month Rowan got her paycheque, took it to the bank and transferred a chunk of it to Tif's bank account in the city. "Don't think of it as a loan," she teased, "think of it as my way of bribing you to stay down there, out from underfoot all the time."

"I'll pay you back," Tif promised. "Someday. Somehow."

The once-a-month Sabbath family feasts became twice-a-month, and then, predictably, once-a-week. And everyone heard regularly how unfair it was that everyone was willing to send money to Tiffany so she could sit on her bum in school forever and nobody seemed to care that Alys never had enough money to make ends meet. "What I'm doing is just as important as going to school and learning about some dusty old prehistoric civilization!" she snapped.

"Right," Rowan agreed, "and the government hauls taxes out of my wages until it's hardly worth getting out of bed, and those taxes go to pay your welfare cheque. Those are *your* kids, Alys, it ought to be up to you to do something about them. I wasn't there for the laying of the goddamn keel, why should I have to underwrite the launching?"

"Oh, fun-nee, Rowan. Fun-nee." Alys lit another tailor-made ciga-rette, and managed to inhale deeply and pout at the same time. "This house is so big," she veered back toward square one, "that we could all . . ."

"No," Rowan interrupted firmly, barely able to keep anger from sharpening the sound of the word.

"I think you're just being stubborn and mean!"

"No!" Sue didn't care how much anger throbbed in her voice.

"Some grandmother you are!" Alys shouted. "You don't even care that we're living in a mingy little auto court with no yard except the parking lot."

"Tell you what." Rowan stood up, her face hard, the nerve under her left eye twitching slightly. "You pack up the kids' stuff and move *them* in here, while you go back to school and learn how to feed your own self."

"So they're welcome but I'm not!"

"Something like that," Rowan snarled. "Because right behind you seems to be a bloody endless string of misfits, ne'er-do-wells and drunks. But if you decide to go back to school and do well at it, or to sign the kids over permanently, there's plenty of room on the second floor for them."

"You just go to hell!" Alys sobbed.

Instead, Rowan got her rowboat and oars, heaved it all into the back of the pickup and headed out onto the chuck to work off her fury.

Justin and Laura split up for two months, then there was a big kiss-and-make-up and he moved in with her again. They didn't get married because that would interfere with her welfare cheque. When Sue suggested that what they were doing was fraud, Justin laughed and shrugged. "Hey," he said easily, "I'm not the one on welfare. That's not my concern. All I do is look after me. I go to work, I get my pay, and if I leave some of it around where someone can pick it up to help pay her rent and groceries, where's the crime in that? Are they my kids? Anyway," and the grin disappeared, "without my pay she can't live decently on what they give her." Several months later, he and Laura had another big fight and he moved out for a month, but then one or the other or both of them got lonely, and the off-again-on-again was on-again.

"I don't mind that I'm at work all day when the soaps are on," Sue shrugged, "I can just pick up the phone and dial their place and I'm up to my ears in As The Stomach Churns."

"Some people don't know they're alive unless they're adrenalized, I guess," Rowan agreed. "Maybe you can get as addicted to stress as to cocaine."

"I'd like the chance to get addicted to boredom."

"Yeah, let's hear it for boredom!" Rowan stood behind Sue, put her arms around her waist, her palms flat on Sue's belly. She hugged gently, and kissed the back of Sue's neck. "Although I have to admit," she whispered, "that one thing *you* don't make me feel is bored."

"Why am I doing dishes? Why am I standing at this sink with my hands in soapy water when I could be doing something altogether else with them?" The dishwater was very cold and very greasy before anyone paid further attention to the dishes.

Alys's fourth pregnancy did not go as smooth as duck shit on fresh-cut grass. She spent most of her time lying on the sofa with her feet up, and the kids learned to pull on their jackets, take the youngest by the hand and make their way over to Grandma's house. They got better at predicting Rowan's days off and Sue's shifts at the oyster plant than Alys herself, and it was nothing for them to come home from work and find the kids in the TV room, grinning over a pile of apple cores and orange peels.

When the baby arrived, Alys had a homemaker for a month, but her baby blues just got deeper. Sue and Rowan tried hiring someone to go to the apartment and "do" for them all, but the kids didn't care for that arrangement and as soon as Brit and Ty came home from school, they'd haul Dee's jacket on and drag her along the sidewalk, down the alley, through the back gate and up the stairs. Brit would haul her key-on-a-string out from where she wore it against her skin, unlock the back door and they'd be there, playing music or watching TV or cutting magazines to confetti with scissors, when the first one got home from work to start supper. Sometimes it was Sue, sometimes it was Rowan, the kids didn't seem to care which.

And one evening Rowan came home from work with a big bag of groceries, walked past the climbing rose bush where old Babe was buried, went into the house and found Brit with the baby in her arms.

"He doesn't feel good," she declared, shoving him at Rowan. Rowan put the groceries on the counter and took Chuck before Brit shoved him through her. Brit turned back to the television.

"What's wrong with him?" Rowan asked.

"I don't know. He's all snotty and he throws up all the time."

"Where's your mom?"

"I don't know."

"Well, where was she when you got home from school?"

"I don't know."

"You mean this kid was at home alone?"

"Don't be silly, Rowan, Dee was with him." Brit shook her head as if she could not believe how thick Auntie Rowan could be sometimes. "I think Dee's sick, too," she added.

The doctor said it was a virus and gave Rowan a prescription. Sue went over to see why Alys wasn't looking after her son herself, and the apartment was empty. She came back home, her face white. "Where's your mother?" she asked, and Brit shrugged. So Chuck spent the night on a nest made from the cushions off the sofa, on the carpeted floor next to Rowan and Sue's bed. Every time he coughed, Rowan jerked awake, her belly tight with the fear the kid would choke to death.

He didn't. He got better, Alys turned up again, Sue raised the roof and promised the next time the kids were left alone she was phoning the welfare and having them apprehended. Alys wept and wailed and declared that the whole world was picking on her, and the kids went home for a couple of weeks, although as often as not they were waiting for supper. Then Alys effed off again and the kids stayed full-time for three days, with a sitter for Chuck and Dee while Rowan and Sue were at work.

"If this doesn't stop," Sue yelled, "I'm phoning the welfare and turning you in! Grow up, Alys, will you? You've got four kids, you can't just bugger off when the whim hits you!"

"You never did understand!" Alys screeched. "All my life all you've done is ride my case!"

"I'm warning you, this has got to stop. You leave those kids alone like that and the next thing you know they'll be in a foster home and you'll be sitting in an empty apartment."

"I don't care! I'd be better off! They'd be better off! We'd all be better off!"

"What the fuck is this, an English lesson?" Rowan roared. "I snivel, you snivel, they snivel, we snivel, we have snivelled, we will snivel, parse it forward, parse it backward but don't *do* a fuckin' thing?" Alys gaped, Sue gasped and Rowan hit her stride. "It's the screwin' you get for the screwin' you got, kiddo! As simple as one-two-three. You wanna fuck, you use birth control. You don't use birth control, the stork drops a package down your chimney. When you fuck with men, the question is not Will I get pregnant, but When! So just pull up your pants, cross your legs, and give your poor, underused fuckin' head a shake, because if I get any more pissed off it won't be the fuckin' welfare you have to worry about, it'll be *me*, comin' through your goddamn door and poundin' the livin' shit out of you!"

She scooped up the sobbing Chuck and set him on her hip where he clung to her, his fists knotting her shirt, his slobbers making little snail tracks. Alys had heard all she wanted to hear, had heard, in fact, more than she had ever wanted to hear, and just grizzled, snoffled, minged and whined on about how nobody, in all her life, had ever so much as tried to understand her.

"You're always against me," she screeched. "You never did take my side in anything!"

"Side?" Sue screamed. "What side, Alys? Who's against you? Who's the one who's ruining your life for you? Near as I can see you're the only one involved in this, and you're the one buggering it up for us all!"

"See? Didn't I tell you?"

"If I say black you do white, if I say green you do red, if anybody at all said the house is on fire you'd run into it or sit down and refuse to believe the flames were hot! You're your own worst enemy, but it's always someone else's fault. And I am through feeling it was something I did or didn't do that is at the root of your bullshit. *Your* bullshit!"

For all the good any of it did, Sue and Rowan might as well have gone outside and banged their foreheads against the edge of the steps. Alys was getting more of whatever twisted thing it was she wanted by being a loser, than she knew how to get as a winner.

"Too bad we couldn't just ignore it for a decade or so," Tiffany sighed. "But I guess that would mean ignoring the rug rats, too, and they'd probably starve if we did that."

"They wouldn't starve," Sue corrected, smiling sadly. "They're too much like you were. Before they'd starve they'd pull a bank job."

"With Chuck driving the getaway car, I suppose," Tiffany laughed.

"How can you make sick jokes about it?" Rowan breathed. "It's awful!"

"Sometimes," Sue said, patting Rowan's hand reassuringly, "you either make a sick joke or you start screaming. And if you start screaming, you might never stop."

"I used to think it was my fault," Tif confessed, blushing beet red and blinking rapidly. "Alys would get herself into a real snit about something and I'd believe her when she said it was because I'd, oh, whatever it was she said I'd done."

"Your fault?" Sue stared, then shook her head. "Well, welcome to the club. I thought it was my fault for depriving her of the chance to form any kind of bond with your father."

"Bond with him?" Tif laughed bitterly. "Hey, when was he around? I mean with Krazy Glue we couldn't have bonded with him!"

"There you go. If you want to feel guilty, you can always find a reason, I guess."

"I just hope Chuckie has the sense to steal an automatic." Rowan got up from the table so quickly her chair scraped the floor and banged against the wall. "His legs are too short to reach the clutch, and he won't get far in first gear."

"I just hope he's got sense enough to put a brick on the gas pedal," Tif said. "And I don't know what *you're* getting yourself all tied in knots about," she teased, "after all, none of them are blood kin to *you*."

"Thank God."

Justin's job took him to Hazelton for three months and Laura and the kids went with him, even though it meant a change of school for them. A month and a half later, Laura packed her things, loaded them on the bus and headed back to the city, because, she loudly declared, she hadn't any intention at all of sitting in Hazelton, in an apartment, with two kids for company, while Justin spent fourteen hours a day at work. "Then he sleeps for eight hours, which leaves two hours out of the day and he spends half of that driving to and from work!"

She dealt with her boredom and her anger by going on a party. Someone decided the party should move to someone else's apartment. They piled into several different cars and headed off, singing and laughing. The car Laura was in was involved in an accident, and Laura wound up in hospital with a broken leg. "My kids," she wailed, "oh God, my kids are alone." The duty nurse phoned the child help line, the child help line phoned the welfare duty worker and the kids were scooped at two in the morning and taken to a foster home. Laura got out of hospital with a cast covering her entire foot, up to her knee, and a pair of crutches tucked under her arms. She went to the welfare to get her kids back and found it wasn't going to be as easy as all that.

"I have to be in court on Wednesday," she sobbed into the phone, "and I can't get hold of Justin so he'll be there with me!"

"Fuck that shit," Justin slurred when Sue finally reached him. "She wanted to leave, she left. She wanted to go drinkin', she went drinkin'. She wanted to leave 'em alone, she left 'em alone. None of it is my doing. Damned if I'll quit my job just to travel four hundred miles to pull her ass out of the mess she got it in."

Laura was so upset by Justin's attitude she crutched her way down to the bar for a few brew to settle her nerves. In the bar she met some of the party types who hadn't been in the accident with her. They bought her a beer, then bought her another one, and she told her sad story several times. They had a few more brew and, since there was nothing to go home to when the bar closed, she went to a party with them. It was a good one. It started on Tuesday night and lasted until Friday afternoon. Unfortunately, the apprehension hearing was on Wednesday morning, and Laura missed it.

"I almost hate the idea of those kids being in a foster home," Sue said.

"Yeah, but what's the alternative? Aren't they better off there than they would be where they were?"

"I guess I should offer to have them come here, but. . ." Sue shook her head and wiped ineffectually at the tears streaming from her eyes. "Two days after they arrived, Laura would limp up, and a week later Justin would come down, and there we'd be, with it all unfolding under our very noses. It's just," she sobbed bitterly, "I can't stand the idea of them being with strangers."

"Hey, *we're* strangers to them," Rowan protested. "And anyway the post office is still working, the phones still ring. I made it through a lot of years in foster homes because my grandma kept in touch. So we'll keep in touch. A parcel here, a parcel there, some cards, some letters, it adds up. Nobody expects either of us to pull on our aprons and rush off to save the world. And anyway, it's not like they were the little match girl standing in the snow!" And yet she felt as if her last six meals had turned to lead and were sitting in her stomach, pressing against her chest. "We'll just keep in touch with the foster parents and maybe have the kids up for school holidays or something."

"What can I say." Justin even sounded blurred and Rowan wondered what the world looked like to him. Could he see the phone or was he just talking in the general direction of the sound of her answering voice? "I mean, I don't know where the woman's fuckin' head is at. Goin' off like that, leavin' them alone. I got no use for that kind of thing."

"What has she done that you aren't doing?" Rowan countered. "Her drinking is out of control and so is yours."

"Maybe so," he said, sounding self-righteous enough to set Rowan's teeth on edge. "But if I go out and get smashed I'm only hurtin' myself. When she does it, there's those kids to be considered."

"So why don't you sober up and consider them?"

He began to feel sorry for himself and the whole world after him. "It might be you're right. I mean, how can they grow up properly without some kind of male parenting figure, eh? You yourself ought to know about that, raised as you were without the influence of your father."

"I was probably lucky." Rowan felt boredom falling on her head like a ten-ton boulder. Young or old, male or female, rich or poor, good looking or as ugly as the underside of a rotting scow, sooner or later every drunk began to sound like every other drunk. "Considering the fact my mother had a Harley Davidson tattoo, there's a good chance my father was every biker in the Burnaby CatWalkers. That would have been some male parenting influence." She hung up the phone before she got nastier than she already felt.

"I begin to think," Sue said, rubbing soap on the washcloth and kneeling to scrub Rowan's back, "that after a certain age people don't really grow at all, they just become more and more what they've always been. And their ability to hide their flaws and stupidities wears thinner."

The helicopter came in low over the clear-cut, then hovered, the dragonfly body gleaming in the clear mountain air, the whirligig blades strobing across the faded blue sky. On the ground the crew raced to grab the skyhook, guide it, slip it through the huge connection. They went down the side of the slinged heap like mountain goats and pounded from the landing periphery, watched with a kind of weary bitterness as the chopper began to lift, tightening the sling, taking the heap of logs from the ground, raising them higher, ever higher.

"Must cost a friggin' fortune." One of the men spat snoose-juice expertly, and the others knew more than brown spittle was being expelled from his mouth.

"Soon's they can figure out a way to replace us with trained dogs we're on pogey," another agreed. "The fuckers."

"Ain't necessarily going to be dogs they use," another announced. He turned away to hide his grin. "I hear tell in Quebec they got frogs out doin' this kind of work," he added, and the others chortled happily.

They watched as the helicopter rose and the sling of logs cleared the tops of the trees. Then they moved to the next heap of sticks and began to prepare for the next helicopter.

The machine sped from the valley, climbed, moving the mind-numbing load easily, heading down-coast, toward the dry-sort. Slopes once safe from logging simply because they were too high, too sheer, lay clear-cut beneath it, the thin layer of soil drying, already starting to blow off in the constant wind. Slash criss-crossed the rocky hillsides, the once green cedar, fir, and balsam needles reddening, waiting for the hot season to bake them to tinder so lightning could set them off and fire could finish what the corporations had started.

On a weathered bluff some eighty feet above the heaving waves, an old cedar swayed as a second chopper, skyhook dangling, came in low, heading for the valley. Hidden in the greenery, snugged so close to the centre the trunk had grown around the first board, a burial platform, weathered to a pearly grey, shifted fractionally. The cedar twine lashings tightened, and knots fashioned by fingers young at the time and long since dead, strained.

The cough of a chain saw starting up scared the Stellars jays, a raven screeched with fury and flew away. The congregation of whiskeyjacks bopped on the branches excitedly, promising each other bread crusts and bits of bologna sandwiches, cupcakes and twinkies, slices of orange and tossed apple cores. Souls of dead loggers, the whiskeyjacks knew full well what lunch kits were and never hesitated to approach the crewmen even now falling trees.

The agile young logger heard the first groaning crack and stepped back, turned off his saw as he wheeled and moved quickly along his predetermined path, away from the massive tree. He shouted and the rest of the crew moved to safety, stood, awed in spite of their years of watching this very same thing, as the giant shuddered, swayed, then leaned. The sound of heartwood breaking was numbing, the swish as she went down was like the wind of the autumn gales and when she hit, the ground trembled. Trees along her path of fall snapped, branches flew, rocks leaped and rumbled and as the din slowly faded, the men looked at each other, shaking their heads in wonder.

"More than a dollar or two there," one approved.

"Don't see 'em like that much these days," an older man agreed.

The dying tree shuddered and bucked, the branches springing free where they could. More rocks slid, a boulder slipped, one of the snapped neighbour trees fell and the older man spun quickly, grabbing the young faller by the shoulder. "Feet do yer stuff!" he yelled, heading for the safety of the untouched forest, where living roots still clung determinedly to the stable ground. Without asking who, what, when, where, why or how fast, the younger men followed, leaving lunch kits, chain saws, gas cans, and whatever else was there to take care of itself.

The sand and gravel of the slope slithered, and the clear-cut area began to head for the bottom of the mountain. Dead stumps, tangled branches, logs and the dusty coating of thin soil slipped off the face of the rock.

The loggers pelted from the show, heading nowhere except away, moving as quickly as they could. A tough tendril of ground-hugging vine snagged on the glistening caulks in the sole of the near-new boots of the youngest, a blond-haired twenty-year-old third-generation bushwhacker. He pitched forward, his hands flying to protect his face. They heard the bones in his wrist snap, heard him curse vehemently. Before they could slow down and turn to help him, he was back on his feet, still cursing, holding his arm and hand against his chest, thundering behind them. The mess coursed downslope and filled a portion of a small valley, wiping out forever a small spawning stream, depleting the salmon population by twenty thousand fish a year.

"Jesus jumped-up Christ on a blue suede cross but this bastard hurts," the youngster mourned.

"Ah, quit yer bitchin'!" The oldest one pulled his Copenhagen can from his back pocket and held it out for the others to take a pinch before he filled his own bottom lip. "Yer alive, ain'tcha?"

"Must be." The blond stuffed his lip awkwardly with his left hand, pushed the snoose in place with his tongue, turned aside politely and spat quietly. "They tell me when you're dead you don't feel nothin', so I can't be dead."

"If yer gonna faint," the older one said as the colour drained from the younger man's face, "just slide down on yer ass so's you don't bust the other one, too."

"I ain't gonna faint," the kid assured him. "Although," he tried a sickly grin, "I might puke."

Slowly, the old cedar leaned to the sea, the roots pulling inexorably from the earth. Everything beneath the ground was altered by the slide, the balance of survival shifted. Something snapped, then something else, and the old tree jerked. The burial platform shifted and bones fell from between two planks.

Almost soundlessly, she dipped farther and farther over the bluff, and treasures any museum would have fought to own scattered from the disintegrating platform. A small hand-carved cedar box fell from the branches, missed the moss and rock and plummeted to the water. The impact split the box, and everything inside it sank to the bottom. Except for the cobalt blue trade beads on a thin strand of copper wire. The necklace looped around the end of a splintered piece of cedar, caught on a jagged shard and dangled, glittering, in the chuck.

The incoming chopper hovered, and the men came from the safety of the bush and made their way to the edge of the clearing. Minutes later, they were inside the machine, heading back to camp, leaving behind a small fortune in chain saws and other gear.

"Fuckin' hairy way to make wages," one of them mourned. "Maybe I'll just buy me one of them soldier of fortune magazines and get an address or two outta it. I could maybe get me a job in one of them hot places where you can pick fresh whatchamacallits right off the tree and stuff yer face on free food when yer not busy shooting hee-haws up the ass or something. Couldn't be no worse'n this, by Christ."

"Ah, you oughta've been here in the old days," the older logger teased. The others looked at him and grinned. From the height of his thirty years, he winked. They laughed softly. "My first job," he chuckled, "they teamed me up with this old Swede logger started every fuckin' sentence with 'Ja shoo-er, in de oldt dayss'. I coulda plugged his word-hole with a sweaty sock by the end of the first day."

"Ja shoo-er," they agreed. "In the good old days."

"In the good old days," the young blond's voice quavered with the pain in his arm, "I had nothin' to worry about except was my mother gonna have rhubarb pie for dessert or was it gonna be chocolate cake." He leaned his head back against the metal wall of the chopper and closed his eyes, nursing his swollen hand and painfully angled broken wrist against the jiggling and bouncing of the helicopter. "Compy for me, I guess," he sighed.

"And retraining." The oldest of them rubbed his face, then dared to step into another man's business. "Take the retraining," he said firmly. "You can do 'er. Get yourself a job as won't kill or cripple you. Welder or some damn thing."

"Ah, shit," the young man sighed. But he nodded, looking down at the eroding coast that even in his short memory had been a tossing sea of green. "It's a cryin' shame, you know," he decided. "But what's a guy to do, eh?"

The floating piece of cedar bobbed on the waves, was pushed by the wind, dragged by the current and tossed by the tide. Three weeks later a storm shoved it onto a strip of sand, where it jammed between two barnacle-covered rocks. The retreating tide cracked the piece of wood, then snapped it. The trade beads on their piece of copper wire slid into the crack and jammed.

"C'mon, Chuckie," Rowan called, "bring your shovel and pail over here, there's lots of room to dig."

The two-and-a-half-year-old trudged over, his face serious, his feet shoved into a pair of worn canvas slip-on sneaks to protect him from sharp shells, broken glass and the proliferating barnacles. He squatted easily and began scooping sand into his yellow plastic pail, stopping to stare at the tiny crabs he uncovered.

"Careful," Rowan warned, "they can pinch!"

"Pin-ss," he agreed. "Pin-ss ow!"

"Pinch ow, for sure." She sat on some dry rocks and looked over to where the other three were racing around in shallow water, screeching and throwing lengths of bull kelp at each other. "You'll be doing that next year," she promised. Chuck had no time or thought for next year, he was busy filling his pail, dumping it over, emptying it so he could refill it again, his rump resting on the damp sand, his blue shorts faded and worn. He picked up a few pebbles and tossed them, laughed when they splashed in a sun-warmed puddle, then dug some more sand with his red shovel.

Rowan leaned forward to pick up a clam shell, and instead, her attention was grabbed by one of the cobalt blue beads. She picked it up, and the copper strand came free of the covering of sand, disconnected itself from the gripping rocks. "I found something," Rowan told Chuck. He looked over, laughing, saw the beads glinting, and got to his feet. "Easy," Rowan warned, "don't break it."

Chuck didn't even reach out to touch the necklace, he just stared, his eyes round. "Pretty," he decided.

"Very pretty," Rowan agreed. "And one day, when you're old enough to know what this is, and old enough to take care of it, it'll be yours, okay?"

"Yup." He reached out one finger and gently touched a bead, making the entire necklace swing slightly. "Pretty," he repeated.

Rowan carefully stored the beach-gift in her pocket and got to her feet. "Comin'?" she asked, holding out her hand. Chuck took her hand and walked with her to retrieve his pail. He picked it up, sand and all, and headed back to the blanket.

"We leavin'?" Dee yelled.

"Not yet," Rowan assured her. "It's sandwich time for the walking appetite."

"Oh yeah? That's *me!*" Dee raced from the water, the older kids chasing her. "I could eat a horse," she announced, plunking her wet backside on the blanket.

"You get your wet bum off that blanket or you'll die of starvation," Rowan scolded. "I don't know how many times I've told you, don't sit on the blanket when you're wet!"

"Yes, Rowan," they chimed, kneeling in the sand and ostentatiously wiping at the blanket.

"You scatter sand in the sandwiches and you'll be the ones have to chew grit."

"Yes, Rowan," they grinned at each other.

"And don't just Yes Rowan Yes Rowan," she finished. "When I'm nagging you I want you to pay full attention!"

That night, with supper finished, the dishes done, and the kids finally in bed, Rowan had time to really examine her find. "I wonder how old it is?" she asked.

Sue looked at the beads, then at the copper wire, and shook her head. "I don't know, but I bet it's older than the sum total of both of our lives. You could probably send it to the museum in Victoria and they'd maybe know."

"Yeah. Or I could just not bother. I mean, it *is*, you know? However old it is, it *is*, and maybe that's what's important."

"You going to wear it?"

"Think I should?"

"I think you should. It was made to be worn. See how the copper wire is twisted here? No sharp edges to scratch or dig and if you move this one. . . see? It's a clasp. Here, bend your head."

Sue slipped the wire around Rowan's neck, then carefully fit the clasp loops together. "Want me to give it an extra little twist, just to be sure it doesn't come apart?" Rowan nodded, Sue squinted and the clasp was shut. "There you go. Let's see. Oh, wow, it looks great! Looks as if someone made it just for you!"

"Feels good. Feels really good. Thank you." She bent forward and kissed the tip of Sue's nose. "You've got great fingers," she winked, "I bet you could fashion a career with them."

The blue trade beads lay warm against her skin, the soft night breeze through the open window was cool on her bare back. Rowan Hanson lay on her belly with the sheet pulled just over her butt, sleeping with her face turned to one side, safe in the recurrent dream of a place where every child was called "cousin," all the men were "uncle" and every woman not her mother or grandma was her "auntie."

Up-coast, people she would not recognize if they took the ferry and stood in the line to buy apple pie or coffee from her, waited through the long hours of the night, keeping Alice Hanson company, singing songs to help her find her way from this reality, past the curtain which obscures that other reality. Alice opened her eyes occasionally and looked at her children, all of them, the living and the dead, gathered in the room with her, soothing her with their love. A faded photograph of three-year-old Rowan Hanson in jeans and a hand-me-down tee shirt was on the bedside table, in the frame that had come from Woolworths with a picture of Tyrone Power. It looked better with Rowan's photo over top of the other one.

"She'll do fine," one of the dead children whispered, "she'll do fine, Momma, don't worry about her, just do what you have to do and come to where you can keep an eye on her."

"I'd like a drink of water," Alice Hanson whispered. One of the living children rose quickly, moved to the bucket on the sink counter, dippered out a glass of water and took it to her mother. Alice sipped gratefully, even managed a smile. "It's thirsty work, this dying," she said.

They lowered her head back to the pillow, and each time she licked her lips one of her living children spooned water onto her tongue. The first light of dawn was just coming over the horizon, bathing the ugly scars of clear-cut logging on the slopes behind the little cluster of unpainted, weather-greyed cedar houses, when Alice Hanson's spirit left her exhausted body and started on the four-day journey to that place where thirst is unknown and sorrow is forgotten.

Rowan Hanson wakened, her mouth parched, her throat tight. She went to the kitchen and took a big plastic torpedo of root beer from the fridge. She didn't even bother with a glass, she just unscrewed the cap and drank from the plastic jug, her throat swallowing, swallowing, swallowing until she thought her stomach would burst. She didn't quite manage to drain the torpedo. She walked to the window and looked out at the pink glory of the dawn sky. And suddenly, she wanted to cry, to just lean her head against the cool glass pane and sob like a terrified two-year-old. As quickly as the need to cry had hit her, it was gone, and in its place was a feeling of peace. She relaxed and stood quietly, watching the pink fade to first morning blue, the mist dissolving in the warmth of a new day.

Laura phoned after supper one night, half swacked and sobbing into the phone. "If you'd just see your way clear to help me with this," she sniffled, "I'd be so grateful! There's no sense askin' *him* to help, he's got a new girlfriend and every time I phone it's Patty Pat-a-cake answers, not him. And I need someone to show up in court with me and put in a good word or two, you know."

"I'm afraid I can't do that," Rowan said firmly. "You walked out of the treatment centre after only three days, and you haven't gone back.

The last three times you phoned you'd been drinking. In fact, you don't phone when you're sober. So how can I stand up and truthfully say I think you've cleaned up your act?"

"Some kind of grandmother *you* are!" Laura hissed. "You don't care if those kids stay in a foster home forever!"

"I'd rather they were there, with sober people, than living in an ongoing party with people too drunk to know if supper's been cooked or not."

"Yeah? Well, look who's talking! The original gearbox herself!"

"Yeah, and your fuckin' mother was another," Rowan agreed, replacing the receiver. She turned and Sue was laughing openly. "What!" Rowan demanded.

"That trick you're learning with the phone," Sue winked, "the hanging up and walking away trick. It's great."

"Fuck 'em all and the horses they rode in on, too."

She almost didn't answer when the phone went off at six-fifteen a.m. It was one of her few chances to lie in bed late in the morning, snugged up against the warmth of Sue's body. Their shifts seldom coincided and all too often Rowan's late lie-in was marred by Sue's absence, her side of the bed cooling rapidly. But she was on days-off, too, and the phone bell was like an enemy. Rowan was angry when she answered it. "Yes?" she snapped.

"I'm sorry to waken you," the voice apologized, "This is Marion Allan, I'm Ashley and Brandon's foster mother."

"Oh?" was the best Rowan could muster.

"I'm calling you because yours is one of the names on the parcels that come here for them. And on the cards." The woman seemed unable to get to the point of the call, and Rowan nearly suggested she get the sock out and get on with it. "I haven't contacted the welfare yet, but I will. It's just that I wanted to have a clearer idea of what to tell them when I did phone."

"Tell them about what?"

"We're supposed to be leaving on holiday today. And it was supposed to have been arranged that the kids' mother would pick them up the day before yesterday and have them with her for two weeks."

"Let me guess," Rowan sighed, "she didn't show."

"No, she didn't. And then last night she called, after midnight, and, well, I'm afraid she's in no shape to travel."

"She's smashed, right?"

"Yeah." Relief was evident in Marion Allan's voice, maybe because she hadn't had to be the one to name the condition. "I suppose," she said doubtfully, "we could just toss their packs into the back of the station wagon with our own, but. . . our kids are only coming with us as far as their grandparents' place, then my husband and I are going on holiday alone."

"Wow," Rowan laughed softly, "you might even get to talk to each other without being interrupted."

"We're hoping we can still think of something to say to each other. Tommy says he's not sure he remembers how to finish a sentence," Marion laughed.

"You know that once Laura starts screwin' up she just keeps on screwin' up and there's no use trying to be accommodating because she'll just take advantage until you're so fed up you're ready to split her head."

"I'm ready to split her head." The voice trembled, but not with sorrow. "And it's a shame because these kids are trying so *hard*."

"So what have you got in mind?"

"I don't have anything in mind. I just have to figure something out before nine this morning, when I phone the welfare. I mean, I can hardly ask my mom to take on two extras, especially two she's never seen!"

"She'd do it, though, I bet," Rowan said, and she turned and saw Sue standing in the doorway, face stricken, guessing accurately what was being said on the other end of the line. Sue looked away and headed for the coffee machine, and as Rowan listened to Marion Allan, she watched Sue. And suddenly, she knew, as clearly as if someone had whispered the truth in her ear, that on her own, Sue would have had a very different approach to a lot of things. Except for Rowan's oft-stated reluctance to be buried in toys and bits of broken bicycle, there would have been no need for Ashley and Brandon to even be in a foster home. She probably would even have changed their names to something normal and decent, like Lee and Don, names people could feel easy with instead of names heard only on afternoon television.

"Tell you what," Rowan suggested, watching Sue measure coffee into the filter, "there's a bus connects with the ferry. It leaves the Vancouver bus depot at eight. If you can get them on that, all they have to do is not fall over the side into the chuck. Tell them to stick close to the driver and they'll be fine. I'll pick them up at the bus depot here." It was like walking down a hallway and winding up with spider webs tangled in your hair. You couldn't just take it off, you had to make sure you got each individual piece, each strand, and it stuck like glue.

Sue turned, her face white, and stared. Rowan winked, then drew her finger across her throat and the colour flooded back into Sue's face. "You'd better let the welfare know about the switch," she suggested, "otherwise the RCMP'll be running around in circles chasing their own horses looking for them. And tell them to phone me because number one I don't want Laura knowing the kids are here, and number two I don't want Laura knowing the kids are here! She's apt to show up half-packed, looking for them, and if she does, I might just have the mental breakdown I've been trying to find time to schedule for the past four years."

"Listen, if you find time and get it scheduled, ask them to reserve the bed in the rubber room next to you, I'll need it before today is finished. I mean, my God, eh?"

Lee and Don were obviously frightened when they came down the steps from the bus. They looked like two people who expected not to be met, two people who would have to figure out how not to be lost for the next twenty years. Then they saw Rowan and Sue and the relief on their faces was so huge Rowan could have puked with the memory. She saw on the outside of their faces what she had so often felt on the inside of her own.

"Hey, there," she said casually, as if every day of her life she spent several hours on the phone rescheduling her shifts and calling in old favours owed. "How you doin', Smoocheroonies?"

"Hi!" Don rushed forward and hugged her tightly, his face pressing against her belly. "Hi, Nanna."

"So I finally get you for holidays. Lucky me." Sue was hugging Lee, already firmly entangled in the spider's web. And loving every minute of it.

Of course they settled in like two farts in a mitt, and of course the two weeks passed all too quickly. Rowan began to feel like the captain of the rowboat that took the dead across the river. She pulled her oars until she dreamed of pulling them at night. She took kids over to Dinner Rock to show them where the boat had been wrecked, she took kids to Rebecca Reef to mooch for cod, she took kids to Hole in the

Wall, she took kids places she hadn't bothered to take herself. She let Dee have a try, she let Lee have a try, she teased them she didn't know Dee from Lee. She gave Don a try, she gave Brit a try, she gave more tries than she thought she'd ever have the patience to give tries, and they all caught fish, then insisted on helping clean and cook them.

"You're a good sport," Sue whispered, lying with her head on Rowan's breast, one leg across Rowan's body.

"I'm crazy."

"Ah, but it's fun crazy. It's nice crazy. It's decent crazy."

"Yeah, that's what they tell you so you'll get sucked into doing it."

"I love you, you know."

"I love you."

"Yeah, I know. If you didn't we wouldn't be exhausted!"

"I'll be glad when they're gone."

But she wasn't. She knew them, now, on her own terms, on their terms, without a shambling power-tripper to spread slime all over everything. "Of course," she said easily, "any long weekends or holidays you just have Mrs. Allan toss you into the baggage bay under the bus, and one of us'll come down and bail you out when you get here."

"Christmas, too?" Lee hazarded. Rowan looked at her and knew the kid already understood all too well how miserable things would be if they tried to jolly ho ho ho with Laura.

"Bah, humbug," she whispered, leaning to kiss Lee's tanned face. "Bah, humbug to you, Smoocherooni."

"Love you, Nanna."

"G'wan, you do not. No more than I love you. Now get on the bus or the guy'll drive over top of us."

Tourists came and tourists went, cars drove onto the ferry, people parked them, climbed out, locked their doors and lemming'ed up the stairs to the cafeteria to buy wretched coffee and dreadful sticky buns, then sit stuffing their faces. Rowan worked her shifts, enjoyed her time off, helped Sue with the garden in the back yard and went out in her new rowboat to catch fish. Life slipped by as slick as deer guts on a doorknob.

And then Dee's father came back into the picture.

"Alys," Sue sighed, "it didn't work out with this guy last time, why . . ."

"We weren't ready," Alys said calmly, "We didn't know what a good thing we had. But we've both grown up a lot since then, we've both matured."

"When did that happen?" Rowan asked mildly. "I seem to have missed a few chapters in this soap opera."

"Shut up." Alys was as placid as a statue of the Madonna. "What would you know about it anyway?"

"It's like the old song," George smiled, "you never miss the water till the well runs dry, right? Alys and me, we had some stuff to work out but we did that and now it'll be fine."

Sue looked at Rowan, Rowan looked at Sue, and neither of them dared look at either Alys or George.

At first, George was content to move in with Alys and the kids, but less than a month later he was insisting they all move. "That place," he scorned, "Christ, it's as crowded as a sardine can. You can't hardly move for kids! People comin' and goin' all hours of the night, and half the time they're yellin' and hoo-rahin' outside your window, the other half the uproar is goin' on above your head. Who needs it, right?"

They moved from the apartment to a carpenter's special on the edge of town. The kids could no longer just bop over to visit. They could take the bus if they had bus money, but they didn't always have bus money, which meant one or the other would phone and hint around until either Sue or Rowan agreed to drive over and get them.

"Well, it's okay this time," George decided, "but next time you should maybe check, okay? They might not have permission."

"Permission? Alys has never objected. She always seemed to feel the kids could spend as much time with their grandma as they wanted."

"Yeah, well maybe, but that was before, right, and this is now, right?"

"Oh. Right," Rowan nodded. "So you want we should phone back and ask if it's okay for us to come and get the kids after the kids have phoned us and asked us to come and get them?"

"Right," George said coldly, his eyes telling her he knew full well she was mocking him. "Because sometimes the little Christers don't ask permission to use the phone before they start dialling. However," and his tone deepened slightly, "I'm sure they will from now on, if you know what I mean."

"Right," Rowan agreed. "Sure."

"Alys has always been kind of what you'd call permissive, I guess." George continued to stare at Rowan, a slight smile marring his face.

"And the whole lot of them have kind of grown up thinking they're in the driver's seat. Which they ain't. So sooner or later one or all of 'em step in it, and wind up finding out about the hand of guidance being put down on the seat of discipline, if you get my drift. And when that happens, they hit the beeper and their grandma bails 'em out, which, as you probably know, doesn't help anyone very much. I mean either they're getting disciplined or they aren't, right? So if you phone before you head over, things'll work out better, maybe even save you a trip for nothing."

Rowan nodded, then looked over at Alys, but Alys just dropped her eyes and stared at her fuzzy pink slippers.

The next move took them even farther out of town, and the move after that had them sixty miles away and able to visit only on the occasional weekend. Dee seemed totally puzzled. She tried to talk to Rowan about it but couldn't quite explain what was troubling her. "He's my dad, eh, and he loves me. He said so. And I love him! I do! He's my dad! It's just that I don't think he likes us. Well, he likes me, but, sometimes..."

"Sometimes you think he doesn't like the other kids?" Rowan guessed.

"Yeah. He's always spankin' the boys. And sometimes..." Her lip quivered and she looked down at the floorboards. "Sometimes he takes off his belt and he really whales on them. Especially Chuckie."

"He uses a belt on Chuckie? Chuckie is only three and a half!"

"Daddy says Chuckie is bad," Dee's voice quivered. "Daddy says Chuckie is a spoiled little fuckhead."

Rowan went to the welfare office and asked to speak to a child protection worker. She had to wait a half hour, then was shown into a small office with a big desk and two chairs. It could have been the very same office she'd known as a kid. Any of the offices she'd known as a kid. The ones where someone you didn't know told you what other strangers had decided about you and for you. She explained to the worker what the situation was, what Dee had told her.

"Have you seen any evidence of beatings?"

"Some bruises. But they said he'd like, fallen down the stairs, or been jackassing around on the bed and bounced off it, and he's the kind of little whipper who does things like that, so I didn't think too much about it. He's the youngest and he's been trying all his life to keep up to the other kids, so sometimes he tries to do things he just isn't old enough to do."

"Has he said anything?"

"Chuckie hardly ever talks. He was late to start talking, and he no sooner started than Alys and George got involved again, and..." Rowan took a deep breath because her voice was quavering too badly for her words to be easily heard. "And Chuckie hasn't hardly spoken since."

The welfare worker took notes, the phone rang, the welfare worker excused herself and answered the phone. When she finished the phone conversation, she took some more notes, asked some more questions, then put her expensive ballpoint pen on the green blotter covering the top of the oak desk. "When we get a report of a Child At Risk," she said carefully, "we are required by law to do an investigation. And we'll do one. But you have to be prepared for the fact if these children don't confide in the worker..."

"Could I be there? Or their grandmother? They'd talk your ear off, then."

"I'm afraid that might be construed as 'coaching'. But we'll definitely investigate. Often just the investigation is enough."

Rowan went home feeling as if she had just wasted two and a half hours of her time and the welfare worker's time. There would be an investigation, but she knew already what would happen. Crazy George wasn't so crazy he couldn't pull it all off and seem sane as hell. And when the investigation was over, there would be no need to be the least bit sane. He'd haul the kids up in front of his chair and sit there like a Supreme Court judge, then ask who'd been tattle-taling about private family business. Then they'd all eat shit sandwiches, and probably the boys would get double helpings, for no reason other than they were boys. Rowan wondered if that was why so many wonderful little boys got turned into lugans and dippers. Maybe all that stiff upper lip and spare the rod and spoil the child was the way smoocheroonies got turned into statistics. Ninety per cent of all violence in society is done by men. If enough Chuckies learned early enough not to talk about anything to anyone, you'd have an army of silent assassins.

Sue had early shift at the oyster plant, so Rowan drove the kids back after that visit, determined to have a talk with George. She parked the car, got out, opened the back door to let the kids out and walked with them to the rundown house that stood alone on what had once been a marginal farm. George sat on the porch and grinned in her face. She knew he knew she knew, knew even that he knew she knew he knew she knew.

"I hope," he said with a grin that reminded her of a dog with rabies, "that the kids behaved themselves."

"Oh, yes," she nodded, feeling suddenly as if she were five years old again, walking toward a new foster home, which she knew in her little heart would only turn into another unhappy situation.

"That's good. Glad to hear it." He patted the bench beside him and Rowan sat down obediently. "We must be making progress," George nodded satisfaction. "At first, you see, we had every kind of behaviour around here except good behaviour. We had whining, we had complaints, we had lipping off, we had little fartsacks with big ideas about independence. And that doesn't cut it in the world today. Not in this day and age it doesn't."

"Tell me," she invited, almost choking on her pleasant tone of voice.

"What it is," George grinned, with that goddamn grin of his again, "is that obedience is what gets us through life. And if we aren't obedient we get punished. Sooner or later, one way or the other, disobedience brings punishment and it doesn't matter how far you run, or how fast you run, if you've got it coming to you, you get it."

"Really?"

"Yes. You take me. I was sinful and rebellious and I gave in to the temptations of lust and God set out to punish me. Well, I ran here and I ran there, and I dodged this way and I dodged that way, but the whole time I thought I was getting away with something, the whole time I thought I was avoiding the punishment of God, I was being punished. And I was too blind to see it, too deaf to hear it, too puffed up with my own vanity to know it. But I was being punished because that whole time I was denied the chance to have any influence on the upbringing of my daughter. And that was a punishment. Not only to me, but to Dee, because the sins of the fathers will be visited on the children even to the second and third generation."

"Pretty grim," said Rowan, and what made it grimmer was she had already heard it from Justin, in a different context, but just as frightening.

"Maybe so, but grim compared to what? Roasting in hell? I learned, bad as I was I learned, and it would seem these youngsters are learning, too."

"Yes," Rowan swallowed. "I would imagine they are."

"Of course it's harder with those not of my own blood." George nodded as if he were hearing news from an unimpeachable source. Rowan wondered if he even knew he was listening to himself. Maybe he thought he was hearing the voice of God. "Now at the time I first met Alys, she already had the older two. I got to know them some in the time I lived with them. And I could forgive what Alys had done to those two because, after all, it was all before I came into the picture. Before you have a chance to know Christ and know how he wants you to live, well, there's no way you can be held responsible for the mistakes you made. Once you accept him as your personal saviour, all that is behind you. And I knew that, and I figured, if Christ can forgive me, then that's an example, right? I knew, even then, even as sinful and confused as I was, that if Christ could forgive the most horrible of sins, I could forgive the couple of little missteps Alys had made. I put that aside and accepted them the way I accepted her. She hadn't known me at the time, we hadn't forged our unbreakable bond. It's that young one sticks in my throat." He looked at her, and for a minute he looked so frigging sane Rowan thought she had gone nuts. "You see, Alys had met me, had known me, had lived with me, had given birth to my flesh and blood. And she sinned with another man. And that little devil spawn is there, as proof. And trying to bond with him is difficult, trying to establish a rapport and teach him right from wrong is a challenge and a tribulation God has sent me."

"Like part of the punishment?" Rowan hazarded. "The same as missing all that time with Dee?" She knew hundreds, maybe thousands of perfectly nice people believed what George was saying, and it didn't help any to know those nice people didn't interpret the belief as nutsily as George did. He was as crazy as a shithouse rat. And about five times as mean.

"I was afraid you wouldn't understand," George smiled. Rowan wanted to shoot him, put the whole world out of the misery he was sure to bring down on it.

And he kept talking. Five minutes, ten minutes, fifteen minutes, a half hour, and George talked. He talked of how there was more than one heaven, more than one paradise, more than one realization of infinity, and more than one level of purification and awareness. He talked of the years he had spent reading, studying and attaining many of these levels. "I can look at a person and see the demon riding their shoulder," he said calmly. "Even when those demons cloak themselves, I can see them and recognize them for what they are."

"My, my." Rowan wanted to weep, she wanted to scream, she wanted to vomit, and all she did was just sit there letting George's voice pour over her.

"Some people think they're good, but I can tell right away if they are or not. And most of them aren't. And most of them, they know I can tell who and what they are and what it is in their heart, and they fear me and their fear leads them to hate me. Some of them," and he turned and looked at Rowan, the eye contact so strong she felt she was being sucked into his head, "some of them think I'm crazy." He waited, his gaze fixed on her.

"Yeah, well," she smiled, and surprised herself at how easy it was. "That's the easy unthinking way for them, isn't it? If they can convince themselves you're a few bricks short a full load, then they don't have to deal with the truth about themselves. There is even," she smiled more widely, "one or two of them think I'm crazy, too. Until now I felt real alone in the world, but I feel better knowing they think you're crazy, too, George, because now I know I'm in real good company."

He turned and stared out across the weed-claimed fields. The silence stretched. Rowan knew she could sit there however long it took, that whatever it was she was going to feel about this was on hold, and for now, all she had to do was last one breath longer than crazy-as-a-shit-house-rat George.

Finally George rose to his feet and went into the house. Alys came out to sit beside Rowan. "You okay?" Rowan asked.

"Oh yes," Alys lied.

"You're sure?"

"Oh, yes," and Rowan knew Alys knew she was lying. "We're going to get married," Alys said quietly. "George says that's the good and decent thing to do. He wants more children, and he says he doesn't want any more of them to be born into sin the way Dee was. So we're getting married."

Rowan couldn't think of a thing to say to that. She knew if she opened her mouth to make comment she'd start cursing a blue streak, which wouldn't do any good at all. So she just nodded. At last Alys had found someone else to do her thinking for her, and it didn't seem to matter one way or the other that thinking was nuts. All Alys had to do for the rest of her life was what George harangued her into doing. She who had refused to do anything anyone told her, had chosen for herself the voice she would hear. There was no use looking for the reasons; there weren't any. This was just how it was and would continue to be. Because George wasn't the only nut case.

"And we're going to move, too," Alys confessed. "George wants us to get as far away from Sodom and Gomorrah as we can because . . . well, he says it isn't safe, if you know what I mean."

"If you start to taste salt in your mouth, for Christ's sake run," Rowan warned. Alys looked blank.

"He says it will be a new start. And to make a new start you have to make a clean break with the past."

"So you and he will get married, and then you'll move, but you won't tell us where you're going, is that it?" Rowan spoke calmly, even managed to keep her hands loose, not clenched into fists. "Because George thinks Sodom is me and Gomorrah is your mom?"

"Yes," Alys nodded. "And you have to accept that."

"Right." Rowan stood up and dusted off the seat of her pants. "After all," she said calmly, "it's what God wants, isn't it? And who are we to deny God what God wants."

She walked to the car slowly, wondering if she was possibly crazier than George. She didn't want to get into the car and drive away. She didn't want to pretend that the unbridled lunacy coming down all over the world was acceptable. But her feet kept moving her to the car, and her head refused to turn to look at the decaying house.

"Auntie!" Chuck screeched, and something inside Rowan Hanson froze. "Auntie!" He pelted toward her. He had never called her anything but Rowan before in his life. "Auntie, let me come with you."

"Chuck, you get back here!" George roared. Chuck stopped dead. Chuck stopped as if he had just run full-tilt into a solid brick wall. The colour drained from his face, except for his lips, which were suddenly blue and turning darker blue. He turned and headed back to the house, back to where George was even now reaching to unfasten the buckle of his belt. "I'm coming!" Chuck called. "I'm coming, George."

George's hands moved away from his belt buckle and Chuck raced back to the steps, clambered up them and stood looking fearfully up at the five-foot-seven-inch tower of discipline. "Good boy," George said, nodding once. Rowan was reminded of the way some people talk to their dogs, people who do not particularly like dogs. People who are quite willing to take their dog to the electrocution cage because no matter how often they beat the supreme shit out of it, they cannot teach that dog to love them.

George stood, his thumbs hooked over his belt, and watched. Chuckie stood beside him, head bowed, eyes fixed on the bleached planking of the porch. He looked like a sixty-five-year-old dwarf, shoulders slumped and belly hollow.

Rowan waved, forced a smile, got in her car and drove off down the rutted unpaved road. Her hands on the wheel were steady but something was very seriously wrong inside her head. She could see the road, but she could also see a place she didn't remember ever being. She could see an old-fashioned float plane. She could see people standing, numb with horror, paralyzed with sorrow, some of them weeping, some of them waving goodbye. And she knew the only reason they stood and watched was a combination of their own faith in the connection they had with the child, and the gun on the hip of the RCMP. Which they knew the uniform in boots would not hesitate to use. She could hear a small, thin voice screaming over and over and over and over, "Auntie... Auntie!"

And then she could see the inside of the plane, see a door closing, hear the thin wailing voice smothered by the roar of engines.

The cobalt blue beads around her neck burned, the copper wire dug at her skin. She reached up and moved them slightly, and they clicked against each other. Moving the necklace didn't loosen the copper wire, it seemed to be tight around her throat, not quite choking her. Again she heard the sound of a child screaming with terror, again she heard the voice wailing "Auntie, Auntie..."

And heard, too, the cigarette-ravaged voice of her own grand-mother, saying, "A body only gets one good kick at the can, kiddo, and if you miss, you've blown 'er. So when it's your turn to take your kick, you do 'er because you'll hate yourself forever if you let it pass you by."

The tires kicked dirt, sand and gravel, the car fishtailed madly, the blue beads around her neck clicked against each other as the torquing force of the spin jarred Rowan's body.

And then the car was heading back down the vile road, speeding, on the brink of being out of control, and the pounding of her heart was like the sound of drums, and she knew so many things there was no way for her to know. She knew where Maklamaklata was, and it lived inside her, she knew she'd had an Auntie, and that Auntie had never wanted Rowan to be taken away from her. She even knew there were snapshots of herself as a child, kept where Auntie could see them and direct prayers. And Rowan Hanson knew that without those prayers, nothing would have worked out for her, the welfare would never have agreed to let a kid live with a Bunkhouse Bertha, the fostering would have done to her what it did to so many others, and she'd never have had a chance to see the can, let alone take her kick at it.

The car bounced and bucketed over the rough road, Rowan's body held behind the wheel by the seat belt, the blue beads clicking, clicking with the drums, clicking the way deer hoof anklets click. She knew why Chuckie had called her Auntie, and she knew nobody was going to shoot taxpayer-purchased bullets at her.

She slammed to a halt at the foot of the steps, wrenched open her door and started up the stairs, hearing the sound of sobbing, hearing the horrible sound of belt leather against bare, soft skin. "*Chuckie!*" she screamed, and the taste of blood was in her mouth.

The door opened and Chuck catapulted toward her, arms outstretched, face red and off-balance, one cheek swollen, already bruising, his mouth bleeding, his eyes wide with fear and pain, streaming tears, nearly choking on his belly-deep sobs. She swooped him up, sat him on her hip and turned back to the car.

"Get back in the house, Chuck," George shouted. Chuck gripped onto Rowan, his baby body shaking, his teeth chattering with total terror. From his throat came a deep *uh uh uh*, a grunt of something more agonizing than physical pain. Rowan knew she was listening to a mind trying hard not to break into small pieces. "You hang on, Chuckie, it'll be all right. I promise you, Smoocherooni, you're going to be fine."

She opened the car door, put Chuck on the front seat and heard George coming down the stairs after her. She turned, closing the door. Behind George the other kids cowered, wide-eyed, in the doorway. From inside the car the *uh uh uh uh* continued, and she could hear Chuckie's teeth chattering.

Rowan Hanson didn't say a word. There was nothing to say that

George would hear, not a word in any language the mad bastard would understand. She called on all the muscles she had developed over the many hours of pulling on a set of rowboat oars. She just pole-axed the sucker.

The other kids came out of the doorway, down the steps and into the back seat. Brittany hit the door lock on one side, Ty slammed the lock on the other side and Dee sat shaking between them.

"Alys," Rowan said, almost gently, "you do whatever you want to do. You want to come, come."

"No." Alys shook her head, as nuts as the loonytune who was trying to get to his feet at the foot of the stairs. "No. I'm staying."

"They're coming with me," Rowan said coldly, and she knew that even before she took the kids home, she would take them to the welfare, to tell their story to the video camera, which would record for all the judges and for all time the softball-sized purple swelling on Chuckie's face, his broken jaw.

"Yes," Alys agreed.

"And staying with us."

"Yes," Alys nodded and Rowan knew with a sick certainty that something in Alys had snapped, and she would probably find a way to off herself very soon.

"No," George vowed, "no, they won't!" He rolled to his belly, pushed with his arms and was halfway up to his feet when Rowan Hanson took her once-in-a-lifetime kick at the can. George's can. Her grandmother was helping her, more people than she knew she had known were helping her. She felt as if with that one kick she had knocked the world right off its axis and changed the course of several human destinies. George gasped and fell on his face in the dirt.

"Hurts, doesn't it, asshole," Rowan said pleasantly.

And then she got in the car and drove home, back to Maklamaklata, the blue beads a circlet of warmth and approval around her neck.